HER ALIEN LIBRARIAN

STRANDED ON EARTH

BOOK TWO

IVY KNOX

Cover art: Natasha Snow Designs

Edited by:Tina's Editing Services, Mel Braxton Edits, & Owl Eyes Proofs & Edits

❋ Created with Vellum

AUTHOR'S NOTE

If you don't have any concerns regarding content and how it may affect you, **feel free to skip ahead to avoid spoilers!**

This book contains scenes that reference or depict sexual harassment, rape mention, caring for aging parents, Alzheimer's, parental death, grief, ableism, racism, homophobia, cops abusing their power, as well as graphic violence which may be triggering for some. If you or someone you know is in need of support, there are places you can go for help. I have listed some resources at the end of this book.

CHAPTER 1

SAMANTHA "SAM"

I refresh my emails one more time as I walk through the Manchester Regional Airport, away from my arrival gate, hoping that a new job had come through in the last twenty seconds, and I can just hop on the next flight out of here.

There's nothing, and my heart sinks. I get in line at Dunkin' Donuts and lean heavily on the handle of my suitcase, sighing as I take in the painfully familiar sights around me—the sand-colored floor tiles and the quiet clack of heeled shoes walking across them, the sharp smell of cleaning products, and country music blaring from the only bar/restaurant on this side of the security checkpoint.

Most of the time, I appreciate how small this airport is. The lines for the bathroom are never long, and I can always find an empty seat near my gate. But today, the lack of crowds at MHT bums me out. Being here means it's time to go home. I can't avoid it any longer.

After I've sucked down a large caramel iced coffee in four gulps, I head outside into the muggy spring air and call a Lyft. I can practically feel my hair pulling itself into a ball of frizz as the humidity envelops me. It's not as bad as the moisture in the middle of summer, but late spring humidity in New Hampshire is powerful enough to destroy a woman's blow-out the second she leaves the salon.

Still, there's something about the constant smell of rain this time of year that puts me at ease.

I could've asked Vanessa to pick me up, or either of my siblings, but another half hour of quiet is too good to pass up. My brother and sister would give me the latest on Mom's health, which I already know is rapidly deteriorating, and Vanessa would pepper me with questions about Mylo, demanding I give her more details about the night we spent together.

I'm not ready to go there. It takes all my energy to not think about that night. Most of the time, I can keep the thoughts of Mylo at bay. When I'm lying in bed at night, however, it becomes impossible.

I can practically still feel the tight grip of his hands on my hips as he pulled my body against his. The heat between us when we left the club and found the nearest motel was consuming, primal. We were tearing each other's clothes off even before the door was shut, and we didn't sleep a wink.

My memories from that night have certainly kept my vibrator busy—to the point where I need to charge it daily—but I haven't been able to sleep with anyone else since then. It's been over a year, and I can't get Mylo out of my head. He's ruined me for other men. And the worst part is that I was sure I'd never see him again.

After my divorce five years ago, casual sex was my reprieve. It was simple, uncomplicated, and kept me from feeling lonely. I'd drive to Boston, go out to a club, find a guy to hook up with, give him a fake name, and we'd have a fun night together before going our separate ways. When I met Mylo, I thought he was just another guy I'd never see again. He also told me his name was Marco.

But, of course, his brother married my best friend, and now it's impossible to escape him. The last time I saw him was when I was last home in Sudbury. We recognized each other immediately, but I successfully avoided his attempts to corner me into a private conversation about our one-night stand.

We had bigger fish to fry at the time, but once we got Axil out of jail and their brother, Luka, hypnotized Officer Burton to drop the murder charges against Axil, there was nothing left to distract us from…whatever it was that lingered between us.

So I left. I took the first photography assignment I could get and ran. That was two months ago.

I can't run anymore, though.

My phone dings loudly in my pocket, and I hastily pull it out to switch it to silent.

Jackie: Mom just tried making pasteles, forgot the recipe halfway through, got pissed, and smashed a coffee mug on the floor. Please tell me your flight has landed and you're on your way here.

Cursing myself quietly in the back of my Lyft, I text my sister back.

Me: Yes, I'm 20 min away.

She doesn't respond, not that she needs to, but the lack of response tells me how frustrated she is. Jackie and my brother Marty have been sharing the load of caring for my mother, and I know it's my turn to step up. They both have kids, spouses, full-time jobs, and their own houses to manage, so I know it hasn't been easy for them.

I'm the only one who is single, childless, has a flexible career, and lacks a permanent residence. I should be the one at home with Mom. The last time I spent the day with her, though, she forgot who I was. Her own daughter.

She looked me in the eye as I handed her a cup of coffee, and there wasn't even a flicker of recognition. It was as if I was a stranger to her. Then she asked what I was doing in her house, and I ran out of the room crying.

It felt like someone had cut a hole in my chest with a rusty knife.

Jackie and Marty have had their share of bad days with Mom, too, and since her Alzheimer's is only going to get worse, I need to be a team player and help out. No more running.

But what if I'm bad at this? What if I mix up her medications? What if I'm not tough enough to watch her slowly succumb to this wretched disease? Apart from being married for a second, I've never had to take care of anyone but me. I've been on my own since I graduated from high school, traveling from one place to the next with my camera in hand. What if I can't be the caregiver my mom deserves?

I send a quick email to my editor, telling him I'm unable to take on any new assignments for the foreseeable future so I can be home with Mom. He won't be surprised by my news. I told him about her diagnosis the day it happened, and I warned him that this day would probably come.

Selfishly, I just hoped this day wouldn't come so soon as Sudbury has never been my favorite place. My hometown is packed with pain and trauma I've repressed and other icky memories I'd like to forget.

Vanessa has always shared my disdain for this town, which is probably why we've remained such close friends over the years despite the various locales our careers have taken us to. I'm glad she's here permanently now because I'm not sure I'd be able to get through this nightmare without her.

However, with Vanessa comes her husband, Axil. And with Axil comes Mylo.

I don't know what to do with Mylo.

He doesn't seem like the relationship type which is good because neither am I. It should make this awkwardness between us fade somewhat quickly, once we can both be open about what we want, but do we even need to have that conversation? Those talks are the worst. Plus, there's just too much on my mind right now to think about how to broach that subject.

My Lyft driver pulls onto Franconia Road, the main street that cuts through the River's Edge condo development, and I sigh heavily as we pass the playground and communal pool. So many memories, most of which include neighborhood kids telling me my curly hair looks like pubes, or white girls insisting I don't need sunscreen because my skin is already brown.

A police car passes us, and I instinctively look away and hunch in on myself. At this point, I'll do anything to avoid the local authorities. Especially Officer Burton. He can rot in hell as far as I'm concerned.

With the condos squished together like an accordion, it can feel like there's no privacy, but luckily, ours is at the very end of the row, hugging the wooded edge of the Sudbury Cemetery. The cemetery was often where I'd run to when this town was suffocating me to death, oddly enough.

"I'm home," I call out once I close the front door behind me and kick off my ratty Adidas Sambas.

"We're over here," Jackie hollers in a flat tone from the living room.

I walk past the cramped '80s-style kitchen with yellow tiles and cherrywood cabinets that we've cooked so many meals in, and through the dining room into the living room on the other side of the main floor. Off the living room is a patio with four Adirondack chairs spread out around a fire pit and a line of dead plants that have been there since last spring.

I leave my suitcase at the bottom of the stairs and find Mom seated in her old dusty-blue recliner, and Jackie next to her on the floral loveseat that's been here since before I got my first period. Mom smiles when she sees me, but the smile doesn't reach her eyes.

She looks smaller than when I last saw her. Much smaller. How can someone shrink so much in two months? Her nightgown is wrinkled in such a way that tells me she hasn't showered today, and the flatness of her usually volumized, curly pixie cut confirms that.

Jackie gets to her feet and pulls me in for an unexpected hug. Despite her petite frame, she's surprisingly strong. "You're on leave, right?" she whispers into my ear. "Tell me you're on leave."

"Mmm-hmm," I mutter back.

"Thank god!" she cheers with a relieved sigh. "Ma, guess what? Sammy is going to be home with you for a while. Isn't that great?"

"Why?" Mom asks, her mouth forming a concerned frown. "Were you fired, Sammy?"

"No, no," I tell her. "Nothing like that. I'm just not taking on any new assignments." I place my hand gently on her shoulder. "You look great, Ma," I lie, pinning Jackie with a questioning glare. "Any updates from Dr. Fisher I should know about? How are you feeling on those new medications?"

"Ay, ese idiota," Mom groans, the rock of her chair taking on an aggressive cadence. "He doesn't know anything."

Jackie clears her throat. "You hungry?" she asks me, nodding toward the kitchen. "We ordered pizza." Then she grabs my hand and tugs me along behind her.

"Sure, I could eat."

Jackie plops two slices of mushroom, onion, and sausage pizza onto a paper plate and shoves it toward me. "The donepezil makes her nauseous, so that's why she's lost some weight. She doesn't like taking it, but you need to make sure she doesn't miss a dose because, on her good days, she'll try to convince you she's already taken it when she hasn't." Jackie rolls her eyes. "I swear, she tricks Marty every time."

I let out a chuckle. "He's always been a sucker. Remember when she convinced him his fish wanted to live in the pond by Cumberland Farms? He carried that belly-up little blob all the way there, thinking it was still alive and just wanted to move into a new body of water."

"Well, we all fell for that shit back then."

"Marty was fourteen," I remind her.

She laughs, the sound filling the tiny house we grew up in. "Oh yeah."

Jackie turns her head toward Mom, and my gaze follows, looking through the rectangular pass-through window that separates the kitchen from the dining room. She sighs. "It's not good," she says, her tone turning grave. "They said we'd get eight to ten years with her, but it's only been four and Dr. Fisher said she's already in the later stages of the disease."

"What the fuck does that mean? What stage is she in?" I ask, my voice getting shakier with every word. I didn't think it could get this bad this quickly. It's only been two months since I was here last. She was having trouble remembering things, but those instances were infrequent enough that it seemed like she had plenty of time.

Jackie's gaze drops to the floor. "There are seven stages, apparently, and she's in stage five, which is considered a moderate-to-severe cognitive decline."

My chest tightens. "So...what, there's just nothing we can do to slow it down?"

"Marty and I have started pulling out old photo albums and going through them with her. The doctor said that could help," Jackie explains, then she grabs a notebook from the cubby above the microwave and hands it to me. "I wrote down everything I could think of for you. This has her medications, the side effects she's experienced with each, the healthy meals we've been making her, stuff we've noticed from her bad days, and things we've been trying to make her feel better when she's confused."

I skim through the detailed descriptions that fill the notebook, pausing to roll my eyes when I come across Marty's doodles. The entire notebook has Jackie's handwriting, but Marty just had to include the transparent cube and the Superman "S" in the margins like he did when he was a teenager.

Jackie, per usual, was extremely thorough in her notes. Though, my brain doesn't have the capacity to read them at the moment. If I really want to understand the jumbled letters in front of me, I need to sit down and go through each paragraph a handful of times. Dyslexia is super fun like that.

"Thank you for putting this together. It must've taken a lot of time," I tell her. Time that I could've been here helping her. Precious time I could've been spending with Mom. I feel like the world's biggest asshole.

"Actually, it's really helped me process the changes in her," she says, running a hand through her shoulder-length, pin-straight hair. "I write it all down before I leave each night, and by the time I get home, I feel like I can let the day go and be with Dan and the boys."

"That's good," I tell her. "I imagine there's a lot you need to shake off at the end of the day here."

Jackie places her hand over mine. "You've got this, Sammy. Don't worry." Then she looks at the digital clock on the microwave and sucks in a breath. "I have to get going." She throws her purse over her shoulder and pulls me in for a half-hug. "There's a stack of books on the coffee table about Alzheimer's if you want to read them. And text me if you need anything, okay? I know it'll take a few days to get used to this, but until you're comfortable, don't hesitate to ask questions."

"Okay, yeah," I mutter in a distant tone, the responsibility of this new role finally sinking in. "For tonight, should I..." I trail off.

"She'll need all three medications once she's done eating. She's still showering and going to the bathroom on her own, but Marty and I stand outside the door in case she needs help."

Jackie bends down to kiss Mom on the cheek. "Be nice to Sammy, okay, Ma? She's going to be here with you all day, five days a week. Then Marty and I will take the other two days, so Sammy can have a break. Got it?"

"Yeah, yeah," Mom replies as she peeks around Jackie to continue watching *Wheel of Fortune.*

"Okay," Jackie says with a shrug as she heads toward the front door. "Good luck, Sammy."

"Thanks," I reply with a wave. Then I take Jackie's seat on the floral couch. "Need anything, Mom? Water? Tea? More pizza?"

"I'll have another slice, but no hovering, okay? You'll drive me insane."

I toss her uneaten crusts in the trash and put another big slice on her plate. We eat together in silence in the living room. I watch her closely as she watches TV. She laughs whenever a contestant guesses the wrong word. Everything about this moment is familiar, and what Mom would normally be doing, but I wonder how many of these moments I have left. Times when she is completely herself and knows who I am.

I clean up our plates when she's done eating, and she doesn't try to fight me on her medicine. Maybe she heard Jackie's warning and knows I won't fall for her tricks, or maybe she's taking it easy on me since it's the first night of me being home. I don't know, and I don't care. I'm just glad when it doesn't turn into a whole thing.

"Need anything else, Ma?"

"Dios mío, I don't need anything. I just want to watch my shows in peace," she hollers as she waves both hands in a shooing motion. "Go settle yourself, child."

After dragging my suitcase up the stairs and down the hall to my childhood bedroom, I drop it on the faded beige carpet. The room looks just as it did when I was here last; the light blue shooting-star comforter still covers my decades-old full-size mattress, long statement necklaces that I'll never wear again hang from colorful thumbtacks above my small white desk, and my lavender walls are still mostly covered in boy band and JLo posters.

It doesn't take long for me to unpack. I made sure the last time I was here that my dresser was cleaned out and all my old clothes were donated, so there's plenty of room for my stuff.

Around the base of the lamp on my nightstand, I carefully line up my hand cream, phone charger, phone holder, lip balm, and a free sample of my favorite perfume—Donna Born in Roma by Valentino, in the same order I keep wherever I go.

Without a place to call home, I've always found comfort in the way I arrange my nightstand and my beauty products in the bathroom when I'm on the road. The location changes, but where I put my lip gloss in relation to my eyelash curler remains the same.

Sadness pierces my chest as I think about all the trips I won't take this year, the exotic destinations I won't get to see, or the aspects of life in those locations I won't get to capture on film, the birds, the people, the food, the weather. But no matter how difficult this will be, I have a duty to my family, and it's not one I take lightly.

To combat the growing sense of dread twisting my stomach, I press the cool surface of the perfume rollerball to my wrist and rub a giant circle on it. Several circles, actually. After I apply way too much on my other wrist to match, I swipe it across both sides of my neck. Breathing it in, I let it carry me to happier memories as I stretch out on my bed.

My phone buzzes on my stomach a moment later, making me jump slightly.

Mylo: *You are home. At last.*

CHAPTER 2

MYLOSSANAI "MYLO"

*S*amantha is typing her response. That is what the dots tell me, anyway. Although, I am certain I already know what she's about to say.

Samantha: *How'd you know I'm home? Does word really travel that fast around here?*

Exactly as I suspected. She assumes that the small population of Sudbury is abuzz about her return. While I am certainly excited about it, I have no idea if that is actually the case.

Me: *Not at all. I can smell your intoxicating perfume from here.*

My brothers prefer the more subtle scents of human females, be it the shampoo they use or the lotion they rub into their skin, but I have had a fondness for Samantha's perfume from the moment I breathed it in. It does not reek of harsh chemicals as so many perfumes do. It is soft and warm like she is, with a floral note that conjures an image of Samantha's lush, naked body covered in daisies.

Samantha: *Forgot about that strong dragon nose.*

My lips form a smile as I read her text. Samantha learned of our true forms after Trevor's death when we thought Axil might spend the rest of his days behind bars. Other than Ryan, Harper's nurse, who delivered Harper and Luka's two children, she is the only human who knows the truth—well, the only one who is not mated to any of us.

But she is *our mate,* my draxilio purrs. *Stop lying to yourself.*

I am doing no such thing, I send back to him.

It has been frustrating dealing with his infatuation with her. The part of me that can shift into a winged fire-breathing monster was certain the first time we laid eyes on her that she was our mate. That was over an entire Earth year ago, and he will not relent.

While I am deeply, intensely attracted to Samantha in a purely physical sense, she is not my mate. I do not wish for any mate, in fact. Someday, I'm sure that will change, but I enjoy my life posing as a single human male who runs the local library—despite the financial difficulties I often face maintaining my place of business.

Human females seem to find me pleasing to look at when I'm in my flightless form, masking my horns and blue skin. This pasty version of me with my sweater vests and spectacles, paired with the fact that I am almost always holding a book seems to align with what many females are looking for in a sex partner.

I do not want that to change. My draxilio can have his little crush on Samantha, but it will not derail my plans to remain free of emotional entanglements.

There is also the fact that Samantha is close friends with Vanessa, my brother Axil's mate. If I were to pursue a romantic relationship with her, my draxilio would be pleased, certainly, but if she chose to leave me, I'm not sure he could handle losing her. If it were to end badly, no matter the reason, life for my brother and new sister-in-law would be difficult, and they deserve nothing but happiness.

My brothers and I are fortunate that Luka was able to use his hypnotic power on Officer Burton to get him to drop the murder charges against Axil, but that does not mean we are highly regarded by Sudbury's top policeman. He has made comments since then about how he does not trust us, and whenever one of us passes him in town, he eyes us warily as if we are violent criminals he is eager to bust.

If he were to discover what we truly are, our lives would be over.

It's easier for everyone involved if Samantha and I remain friends and nothing more.

Samantha: *I thought you liked my perfume…*

Then she sends me one of the happy, floating yellow heads—this one with a wink—and blood rushes to the head of my cock.

Is she *flirting* with me?

Me: *You know I do. I would not have run my tongue over every inch of your skin if I did not.*

I can see her now, her blunt teeth sinking into her lower lip as her thick thighs press together. If this is a fluster battle, I hope Samantha is prepared to lose because I have become an excellent flirt since I first arrived on Earth.

The three dots appear, then disappear almost as quickly.

Me: *Don't tell me you have forgotten. I haven't.*

Samantha: *I've tried forgetting…but I fail every time.*

She is goading me now. I know she's remembering our night together, just as I am. The way our bodies found each other on the dance floor, and the visceral hunger that ripped through me the moment she placed her small hand in mine. It was a hunger that could not be sated with our first dance, or our second, and not even when we left the dance hall, and she begged me to take her against the wall of the shabby motel room we rented nearby.

Over and over that night, I drove into her welcoming body, hoping that by morning, my draxilio would be satisfied enough to let her go.

He wasn't, and he still yearns for her touch to this very day.

I begin typing a response that I'm certain will cause her belly to flip, but she beats me to it.

Samantha: *Do you have plans tonight?*

Suddenly, it is my stomach that is doing the flipping.

Samantha: *Wanna meet up?*

Me: *No plans. Come over.*

Even if I did have plans, they would be canceled immediately.

Samantha: *I'll walk over once my mom is asleep. Should be in an hour.*

Samantha: Are your brothers home? I don't want them to see me sneaking in and start asking questions.

I understand her concern. It is best if we keep this rendezvous a secret from the others.

Me: Zev is here, but has been in his room since he got home from work. Axil is next door with Vanessa, and Kyan won't be home until late. I will let you in through the side door. That's the closest entry to my wing of the house.

Zev is sure to catch a whiff of her scent while she is here, but he will likely assume it is just another female I have wooed.

My palms begin to sweat as the dots reappear on the screen. I get to see Samantha tonight. My draxilio trills deep within my throat. He is very much looking forward to this.

Samantha: Perfect. See you soon.

Time goes by painfully slowly, but two hours after her last text, Samantha shows up at the side door, offering me a shy smile as she steps inside and quietly follows me up the steps to my bedroom.

Closing and locking the door behind her, I turn to find Samantha standing in the middle of my room, her arms crossed over her chest, and looking around at the many books that line my shelves.

She wears a short-sleeved floral dress with buttons that stop at the top of her rib cage. It hangs loosely on her voluptuous form and lands just above her knees. The dress does nothing to accentuate her curves, which feels almost criminal, and my hands flex to tear it off.

Her gaze eventually lands on me, and we both chuckle at the thick tension that fills the room. "So…" she trails off shyly, taking a step toward me.

"So…" I reply, taking a step in her direction. "How is your fam—"

I am interrupted when, suddenly, her lips are pressed against mine and her supple body is in my arms. A groan rips from my throat at the first swipe of her smooth tongue against mine. The scent of her perfume fills my lungs, and I wish to learn the name of it so I can spray it all over my belongings, keeping this part of her here with me always. Her small fingers tangle and pull at my hair as mine dig into the soft globes of her ass.

"Wait," she mutters breathlessly as she pulls away. Gently, she lifts my glasses off my nose and places them on my nightstand. "You don't actually need those, right?"

I shake my head. "No, but I look good in them, do I not?"

Samantha's deep brown eyes swirl with heat. "You look very good in them." She pauses as she tilts her head to the side. "But I've already had this version of you. I want the real you."

My chest tightens with nerves at her request. "You mean you want me to unmask?" Unmasking in front of a human is not something I have done before. It is not something I ever planned to do in front of anyone but my mate.

She is your mate, my draxilio sends me through our mental link.

She is not, I send back.

She already knows the truth, he replies, and I find it difficult to argue that point. Samantha knows I am not human. I suppose there is no harm in letting her see me as I truly am.

"Yes, please," she says and takes a step back as her eyes travel down my body.

I am powerless to say no when she looks at me like that—as if I am a prize she has just won.

Closing my eyes, I let go of the mask I wear every day. Each part of my head and neck relaxes as the pale color of my skin fades to a rich cerulean, and the sensation travels all the way down to my toes. There is a gentle tickling sensation when my horns poke through my forehead and curl back over my skull.

Most of the time, I forget that I am masking, as the practice requires little effort beyond being awake, but there is a deep sense of satisfaction the moment I let it go. It is similar to the grinding of teeth, in the way that it can be happening without me noticing, but once I do notice and actively try to stop, the release creates a feeling of lightness and ease.

"Wow," Samantha whispers in awe. Her mouth hangs open at the sight of me in my natural flightless form. Her hand goes to her chest and rests over her heart. "You are…" she pauses as her gaze drifts over my face and horns, "truly beautiful."

My cheeks grow hot at her praise. It is a relief knowing she is not frightened by me in this form. I did not expect her to be since she was not scared when she first learned what we truly are, but it is difficult to predict human reactions. They are a weak people and easily terrified.

"Mmm," Samantha moans softly as she steps back into my arms and runs her fingers along my cheekbones and jaw. When the pad of her thumb swipes across my bottom lip, I open and catch it between my teeth. She sucks in a breath as she watches me nibble and suck on the tip of her finger until she pulls her hand away and kisses me hard.

We stumble in a clumsy circle as we tear at each other's clothes, and once they are in a heap at our feet, Samantha pushes against my chest until the back of my legs bump into the chair by the window, and I fall into it. "This is how you want it?"

"Mmm-hmm," she says as she climbs onto my lap, straddling me, and holds her soaking wet folds just above the engorged head of my aching cock.

There are many things I want to do in this moment. So many ways I have fantasized about touching her. The countless times I have stroked my cock to the memory of her nipples, their deep brown shade, and the way they pebbled against my tongue that night. The taste of her skin as I planted a trail of kisses across the lower, softer part of her belly, moving down to the downy curls that cover her cunt. But Samantha seems to be in a rush to take me deep inside her, and I would never deprive her of such things.

"Need you," she pants as she wraps her fingers around my cock and strokes down to the base. "Hold the fucking phone," she says, jerking back with a shocked expression. "You have ridges?"

"Yes."

Her look is puzzled, and also slightly enraged. "You didn't have ridges last time. I would've fucking remembered ridges."

"They are part of my true form," I explain. "My ridges are like my horns. I only have them when I unmask."

"Then your true form is officially my favorite." Then she smiles wickedly as she takes me in hand once more.

A hiss escapes me through gritted teeth as I throw my head back and pump into her grip.

As good as it feels, I refuse to allow this pleasure to go only one way. Reaching between our bodies, I insert a finger into her core, then a second when the wet sound of her cunt fills the room.

"Yes," she moans as she starts riding my hand, her breasts bouncing with the movement and putting me in a trance. "Harder."

Thrusting into her, I watch in awe as her eyes fall closed and her long, luminous curls cascade down her shoulders. She is the most exquisite creature I have encountered on Earth, but particularly like this, when she is accepting the pleasure she so deserves to feel.

I see now why I have been unable to find another human female I am interested in having sex with. There have been many that I have bedded over the years, but none like Samantha. Since the night we shared, I have lacked interest in bedding anyone else.

I've shifted and flown down to Boston on multiple occasions in search of a female I find attractive, to whom I would give a fake name and fuck until my body was sated, but none of those excursions over the last year led to anything beyond a flirty conversation at a bar. I could not go through with it, and now I understand why. Those encounters would never compare to the night I met Samantha. And now she is here, wet and wanton and worth the wait.

Though her grip on my cock has loosened, Samantha's very touch brings me closer to release with each breath. If she keeps her hand there, I will spill my seed all over it.

"Samantha, I am...close," I say with a groan, using every cell in my body to hold back.

"No, come with me," she says, her voice a husky whimper. She removes her hand from my cock and looks around the room. "Where are your condoms?"

I gesture toward the nightstand. "There."

She hops up to retrieve one and tears the package open with her teeth. Then she returns to my lap and rolls the condom over my head and down my shaft. "I'm surprised these even fit you."

"They don't, really," I tell her with a laugh.

She notices that the condom stops halfway down and is visibly snug with my ridges practically poking through. I expect her to laugh, but instead, she licks her lips and moves her body closer until the hardened tips of her breasts brush against my chest.

"They work only when I am masked."

Samantha lowers herself, stroking the head of my cock along her folds. "It's okay. I'm on birth control."

I suck in a breath the moment she guides me inside. The walls of her cunt clench around the head of my cock, and a loud, keening cry escapes her lips the deeper she sinks down.

My hand covers her mouth. "Shh," I warn her. "You don't want Zev to hear you, right?"

Her hot breath fans my palm as she shakes her head. Then I press my forehead against hers as I pull her down until she is fully seated. She gasps against my hand as we sit there, completely still, her body adjusting to my size.

"Breathe for me," I whisper, rubbing her back, and letting my hand linger on the parts of her back and sides that roll together. So very squeezable.

Eventually, she relaxes around me, and the sheer hunger that was written on her face before returns tenfold. She places her hands on my shoulders, and the blunt edges of her nails bite into my skin as she holds on and begins to move. The pace she sets is fast, brutal, and we become a frenzy of limbs. The sound of our bodies slapping together meets my ears, and it only adds to the desire that consumes me.

Lifting my hips, I drive into her until my sac tightens and the edges of my vision start to blur. "You feel so good," I tell her, my voice ragged with need. "So good."

She places her hands on either side of my face and pulls me in for a bruising kiss. "Fuck, Mylo," she cries in a whisper-shout against my lips. "Yes!"

Panic sets in as her thighs shake and her cunt flutters around me. She is close, but I worry I am closer and will come before she does. That cannot happen. I reach my hand between us and work my thumb over her clit the way she likes. She moans into my mouth and her limbs lock up as her orgasm rips through her. I follow close behind, coming with her, my seed no doubt filling the pitifully small condom and running down the sides.

Our arms remain wrapped around each other as we come down, and I revel in the feel of her body against mine.

Just as it should be, my draxilio unhelpfully adds.

I ignore him and kiss along her collarbone, enjoying the salty taste of her skin. Then I reach the spot on her neck where she applied her perfume, and I breathe it in as deeply as I can.

The moment she leaves my lap, and our bodies break apart, I am tempted to grab her hand and tug her back to me. I want to tell her to stay. That in a few minutes, I will be ready for another round, a new position, whatever she wishes. But when she starts pulling on her clothes, it is clear she has other plans.

"We can't do that again, okay?" she says as she tugs her ugly dress over her head. "This was a one-time thing."

"Sure," I reply, amused by her obvious denial. I don't think I can keep myself away from her now that I've had her again. Especially knowing she is so close by. But if that is the lie she wishes to tell herself, I shall play along. "Never again."

Until it happens again.

CHAPTER 3

SAM

"Never again," I mumble under my breath for the fifth time this morning as I pour vanilla creamer into my mom's coffee mug. I can't stop thinking about Mylo, and it's starting to piss me off. He's a good lay. So what? I've had plenty of those. Why is *he* so impossible to resist? I know he's an alien—an extremely hot alien—but I should be able to forget him like the rest of the guys I've been with.

"What did you say, Sammy?" my mom asks from the dining room table.

"Nothing, just talking to myself."

It's probably because the sex I'm used to is with guys I'll never see again, and he's just a seven-minute walk through the cemetery. Yeah, that's all it is. Proximity. And a distraction. He's a fantastic distraction.

I sit next to Mom at the oval cherrywood dining room table and place the steaming mug of coffee in front of her. Desperate to think of anything other than the ridges that run along the length of Mylo's mouthwatering dick, I launch into the agenda for the day. "Mom, after breakfast, why don't you take a shower, then we can go for a walk around the neighborhood?"

"Yeah, okay," she replies, holding the mug in her hands as she stares distantly out the kitchen window.

"We'll need to swing by the market on Fisherville Road so I can get cilantro," I tell her. "I'm going to make arroz con pollo in the slow cooker later. Does that sound good? Based on the copious notes Jackie left for me, it looks like that's been a weekly staple."

"It has, but can you make sure there's enough salt in it?" Mom asks, then shakes her head. "I would rather not have my favorite meals at all if they're going to taste like a pile of sand."

I go to defend Jackie, knowing that this healthy eating crusade is a big part of slowing down the progression of her disease, but Mom continues, putting down her coffee mug and flattening her palms on the table. "And I want to watch *Real Housewives.* The New Jersey one. Jackie wouldn't let me because she thought the fighting stressed me out, but it doesn't, Sammy. I'm passionate about the way they stab each other in the back. That's all it is—passion."

I try to keep a straight face, but a chuckle falls out of my mouth. Her longing for rich lady drama is too cute to resist. "Okay, fine. Two episodes of *Real Housewives,* but that's it for today." Jackie will be pissed I let Mom get her way, but I don't care. The woman raised three kids on her own after Dad left. She worked her ass off to provide for us. The least I can do is let her watch her favorite shows.

She squeezes my hand and shoots me a warm smile. "Thank you, *Papita.*"

Of all the things Mom remembers, it's that embarrassing nickname from my childhood. Figures.

After she finishes her coffee, I offer my hand as she climbs the stairs, but she swats it away. She takes a shower, and I stand outside the cracked-open door as I try reading Jackie's notebook, but the letters are jumbled and I can't focus, so I toss the notebook into my room down the hall and promise myself I'll try again later. The doorbell rings just as I hear Mom turn off the water, and I make sure I hear her step out of the tub and safely onto the bathmat before I run downstairs to answer it.

I swing open the door to find Vanessa standing there with her arms crossed over her chest. "Hey, Vanil–"

Vanessa puts her hand up, stopping me. "You've been home for almost twenty-four hours and what, you just forgot to text me? Rude." She steps past me into the house with a pouty huff.

"More like twelve hours, actually, but my sincerest apologies."

"I had to hear about your return from Mylo, you know."

"Mylo?" I ask in a squeakier voice than intended. Clearing my throat, I add, "What did he say?"

"Just that he heard you were home. Why?" Vanessa says, tilting her head to the side and looking at me far too closely. "Is there something else he should've said?"

Christ on a cracker, not this again. "No, no," I quickly reply. "Nothing like that."

Her brow remains furrowed.

I decide to change the subject. "Want to sit out on the patio? It's a nice day out, and you can me tell how that little bun in your oven is cooking."

"Oh, good idea," she says, smiling as she looks out the window.

And I cheer silently as my diversion is successful. "Let me check on Mom really quick."

I jog back upstairs to the bathroom and whisper through the crack, "You good, Mom? Need any help?"

She sighs heavily. "I wiped your ass for years, Samantha. I don't need you wiping mine." Her tone is cutting, but I shrug it off. She's always been a fiercely independent woman, and having her kids wait outside the bathroom with the door cracked must be kind of humiliating.

"Okay, well, Vanessa and I will be out on the patio. Let me kno–"

"If I need anything, yeah, yeah," she interjects, and I can practically see her shooing me away.

I join Vanessa on the patio with two large glasses of lemonade, and the moment she sees me, she licks her lips like a cartoon dog seeing a steak. "Ooh, I love your mom's lemonade."

"Pretty sure Marty made this batch," I tell her after taking a sip.

Marty's batches are just the tiniest bit sweeter because he adds two extra tablespoons of sugar. He always has. "Mom and I are going for a walk in a bit if you want to join us."

Vanessa pulls her sunglasses off her head and down over her eyes as she leans back in our old Adirondack lounge chair. "That sounds nice. How's she doing?"

"Not great. I'm not taking on any new assignments for the foreseeable future so I can be here with her," I explain. "It's not like I need to watch her constantly, but...it seems like we're getting closer to that point."

Vanessa turns to face me. "Oof, that's hard, Samwich. I'm so sorry."

I reach out and give her arm an appreciative pat. "Thanks. I'm glad I get the opportunity to spend time with her, you know, before..." I don't finish the sentence because I don't need to, and also because I refuse to acknowledge the inevitable. "I've been gone too long, you know?"

She takes a big sip of lemonade. "Don't beat yourself up about that. It's your job, and your job just happens to take you all over the globe."

I wish I could believe that, but I've reached a point in my career where I can pick and choose the photography assignments I take, and there have been dozens close to home that I passed on because of that very reason. I should've taken them. That's time with her I'll never get back.

"Enough about me," I mutter as my gaze drifts over Vanessa's face. She's had this ever-present faint smile since she met Axil, and now she's having his baby. I couldn't be happier for her. "How's Baby Vanilla doing?"

Her hand rests reverently on the lower part of her stomach. "So far, so good. I can't go to a human doctor for anything because..." she looks around, making sure no one overhears us, "it's part alien, so Luka's mate, Harper, has agreed to help me during the pregnancy. She's given birth to two of her own, and she's a veterinarian, so she's got enough medical training to oversee the growth of my little monster."

"Don't Harper and Luka live in Salem?" I ask, nervous about what this means for Vanessa. "That's a forty-five-minute drive. What happens if you have an emergency? Or go into early labor?"

"When Harper was last here, she brought her head technician, um, Ryan, I think. He helped her through both pregnancies, delivered both babies, and has cared for those boys ever since. He's the closest thing we have to an alien doctor," Vanessa explains, seeming unbothered. "She brought her boys too. So cute. They're teenagers now. Harper's going to come up every month for a sonogram and will stay at my house when I get closer to my delivery date."

I suppose that's the best-case scenario. "And how's Mama doing?"

"Just tired, for the most part. I've gotten sick a few times, but it's been at night, so I can't even call it morning sickness."

"Psh," I say, waving a hand, "you're creating a life inside your body. Call it whatever you want." I kick my slippers off next to my lounge chair and wiggle my toes in the warm sunlight. "How's Axil? Is he treating you like a queen?"

Vanessa chuckles softly. "Oh hell yeah. Last night, I came so hard, I saw God."

A loud cackle escapes me. "God? Really? What'd she look like?"

"Um," she begins, giggling too, "kinda like Charlize Theron in *Mad Max,* with that no-fuss, societal rejection, apocalyptic vibe."

I nod. "That makes sense. She doesn't have time to style her hair into perfect beachy waves. Girl's got shit to do."

"Exactly," Vanessa agrees, still laughing. "And she wears the same outfit every day to eliminate decision fatigue."

I chew on the inside of my cheek. "Didn't you tell me once that you have a crush on Charlize Theron?"

"Oh yeah, that sounds right," she says, a smirk tugging at her lips. She's quiet for a few minutes before bringing up Mylo. "I don't want to keep harping on this, but since you're home for a while, maybe you and Mylo should grab a bit–"

"Ugh, seriously?" I say, cutting her off. "I'm not interested in dating anyone. You need to let this go."

Mom opens the sliding screen door a moment later, looking thoroughly annoyed. "Sammy, have you seen my car keys? I can't find them anywhere."

Vanessa and I exchange *the* look. It's one I've become very familiar with as I've shared it with my siblings several times. Every stage of grief can be identified in that look.

"Mom, you don't drive anymore, remember?" I tell her gently. "Your license was revoked last year."

She looks off into the distance, unfocused, but I can see the sadness in the lines on her forehead. "Oh. Right."

"But it's okay," I reassure her as I get to my feet. "We don't need the keys anyway because we're going for a walk. You still want to do that, right?"

Eventually she nods. "We can stop by the library. I'd like to pick up a new book."

The library. I wonder if Mylo's working.

"The library, eh?" Vanessa says, her eyebrow curving up as if she's reading my mind. "I'm going to head home for a snack, but you ladies have fun on your walk."

Vanessa hugs both of us before she leaves, and Mom and I stroll along the quiet neighborhood roads as we make our way to the library. I expect to see Mylo manning the front desk when we arrive, but a short, older woman with long gray hair tied back in a loose braid is there instead. A flash of disappointment passes through me, but I ignore it. Maybe it's his day off. Plus, this way, Mom can check out a book and we can get out of here quickly. It's better that he's not here.

The Sudbury Public Library might be the oldest building in town, and it's the most beautiful by far. Built in the mid-1800s, the three-level, red brick building has thick square columns at the entrance, an ornate gold design in the transom window above the main door, and high ceilings throughout.

It has several conference rooms that can be reserved for use, large comfy chairs around the fireplace, and the kids' section is designed like a jungle with an area for Mylo's weekly story time that includes a high-backed brown leather chair and lots of thick cushions shaped like lily pads spread out over the deep blue carpet for the kids to sit on.

Today, there are only a handful of people milling about, which surprises me, even on a weekday. I expected a crowd.

I'm about to follow Mom to the second floor of the library when I hear his deep, velvety voice coming from behind me. "I am really looking forward to this. Thank you so much for coming in," he says to someone.

I whirl around to find him shaking the hand of a woman who is so gorgeous, my mouth actually falls open at the sight of her. Our bodies are similar in shape and size—fabulously fat—with her being an inch taller with a slightly broader chest. Her posture indicates the kind of confidence I possess, and her skin is a deep brown shade with cool, jeweled undertones.

She has long black braids that reach the middle of her back, and several gold braid cuffs are evenly spaced throughout her hair. Everything about her is striking, including her teal cat-eye glasses, hot pink lipstick, and her big wide-set eyes in a warm, copper shade. Eyes that happen to be locked on Mylo at the moment.

"I'm excited," she tells him, reaching for his hand.

"Me too," he says, shaking hers. "Nice to meet you, Charlotte."

"Oh, call me Charlie," she replies. Her voice is low and melodic, and I'm not jealous at all because other women are not my competition, especially when it comes to a man I'm not interested in dating. Not jealous at all.

She leaves, and his eyes widen when they meet mine. "Samantha, lovely to see you here." His gaze drifts to my mother, and he strides toward us, stopping in front of my mother to bow. "Ms. Rodriguez, welcome back. Your beauty grows with each passing day."

His charm is off the damn charts. I'm surprised there isn't a line of women out the door just to talk to him.

My mom's cheeks are as red as I've ever seen them. She giggles like a schoolgirl and says, "Mylo, I insist you call me Elena."

"You two know each other?" I ask, surprised by the comfort between them.

"Of course. Elena is always looking for romance recommendations," Mylo replies as he steps behind the front desk and starts digging through a stack of books that's almost as tall as he is. It's too warm for his typical button-down and sweater vest, so today he's wearing a short-sleeve, light green button-down with tiny blue ducks on it, and a navy bow tie with matching navy chinos paired with crisp white Stan Smith Adidas sneakers.

He's dressed like the biggest nerd in school, but with the kind of muscles all the jocks would envy, and a sense of style made for the runway. And I can't stop my mouth from watering at the sight of his back muscles flexing as he lifts a new stack of books off the floor and puts them on the counter. In the next moment, he's pushing his glasses up his nose, and my thighs clench together. What a spectacular contradiction this man is.

"Want another alien romance?" he asks my mom. "I know I set one aside for you. It's here somewhere."

"How often do you come in here, Ma?"

She ignores me. I'm not even sure she heard me as her expression is still flustered and giddy.

"Ah, here it is," Mylo exclaims as he holds up a book with a shirtless man with green and orange scales on the cover. "This one is by January Bell. I read it last week, and I think you'll really enjoy it."

"Jackie finished the one about the ice planet two days ago, so you will start this one tonight, right *mi'ja?*" she asks me, and a lump forms in my throat.

"You want me to read this to you?"

"Well, yes," she replies. "My eyes aren't what they used to be." When I don't say anything, she adds, "You'll read to me, won't you?"

"Y-yeah," I stammer as I try to find a way out of this. "I mean, sure...except, wouldn't an audiobook be better? A professional narrator is certainly going to do a better job than I ever could."

"An audiobook," my mom says, pursing her lips as she thinks. "It's just I liked falling asleep to Jackie's voice, and I want to fall asleep to yours too. Jackie said it was good for my memory."

Well, there's no way I can argue with that. If it's to improve her memory, I have to do it. Though, I doubt it'll be as pleasant an experience with me struggling to read aloud. It's why I floundered in high school, and flat-out refused to go to college. Hearing me trying to read is a full-body cringe for all involved.

The worst part is she knows this. It's not something we ever explicitly talked about, but I remember my teacher telling her that I was struggling to keep up with the rest of the class. She didn't react well to hearing that, and insisted there was nothing wrong with me. At the time, it felt like she was defending me. I felt supported. But her refusal to acknowledge my dyslexia ensured my continued struggle.

It seems she doesn't remember any of that right now, though. Or maybe she intentionally chose to forget since it embarrassed her.

"Um," I begin, hoping a valid excuse to get out of it will just come to me as I'm speaking. "It's just that…t-the thing, here's the thing–"

"If you'd like, Elena, I can come over and read to you," Mylo interrupts, and even though he's speaking to my mother, I feel his eyes on me.

"Oh no, you don't have to do that," I start to say, just as my mom says, "You'd make a house call to read to me?"

"A house call?" he repeats with a low chuckle. "I suppose that is what a house call would consist of for a librarian, so, yes. I shall make a house call."

Our eyes lock, and in his breathtaking gray irises, I see nothing but empathy and understanding. He knows. Apart from Mom, my teachers, and my ex-husband, Nate, no one else has ever suspected a thing. Not my siblings, friends, or even my colleagues. Within moments, Mylo figured it out, and he's helping me keep this secret.

Why would he do that?

He gives me a single nod, and I feel the tension in my shoulders fade. "If it wouldn't be an inconvenience for you, I know my mom would love to have you read to her."

"Not at all," he replies easily. "I am busy tonight, but I'll come by tomorrow. What time is best?"

Busy? I didn't think he had much of a social life. From what I've heard from Vanessa, he spends his free time reading every book he can get his hands on. Does he have plans with hot Charlie who was in here before?

"She's usually in bed around nine," I tell him.

"Then I shall be there at eight," he says.

"Fantastic," my mom quietly cheers.

She pulls out her library card and hands it to Mylo as he gets in front of one of the computers behind the desk.

After he swipes her card, I notice his brow furrowing as he looks at the screen, but when his gaze lifts to my mom, the look morphs into a brilliant smile. "You're all set. And before you leave, Elena, you should check out my romance recommendation table." He gestures to the display table just to the right of the entrance. She nods as he hands her the book, and she wanders over to the table to browse.

Once she's out of earshot, Mylo leans over the counter toward me. "I wanted to let you know that your mom has several overdue books at the moment. I have waived the fees, but could you bring those back at some point?"

"Oh no," I say, flooded with embarrassment. I'm not surprised she forgot to return books she's borrowed, but it's just another thing in a seemingly endless list of ways I need to stay on top of her. "I'm so sorry. If you can print out that list, I'll bring them all back tomorrow."

"Hey, hey," Mylo says in a comforting tone, "it's okay. There's no rush. Just bring them back when you can."

I swallow, amazed that I'm on the verge of tears over this small act of kindness. Clearing my throat, I say, "Thank you. I really appreciate that."

His gaze shifts quickly between my eyes, then down to my mouth, then back to my eyes again. "It is my pleasure." He starts to step away, but I stop him.

"And, hey, thanks for offering to read to her. You really didn't have to do that."

I expect him to confirm his suspicions and start peppering me with questions. But he doesn't. He just says, "I want to," and leaves it at that.

He hands me the list of overdue books, and I tuck it in my pocket before Mom can see it. Then we go on our way, swinging by the market for cilantro and back home, with Mylo occupying my every thought the entire time. Too many of said thoughts linger on what his plans for tonight could be.

The rest of the day passes quickly and quietly, and after we eat dinner, which, according to Mom "finally tastes like real food," we go through old photo albums together and laugh at the pictures of me and my siblings on Christmas morning, our hair a tangled mess and our pajamas wrinkled as we park ourselves around the tree, holding our most cherished gifts of the day.

Then I let her watch a few episodes of *Real Housewives.* She's the most animated I've ever seen her with this show on. She gasps, shakes her fist, and yells at the TV when her favorite housewife delivers a scorching zinger.

My phone buzzes on the side table as Mom is fast-forwarding through commercials, and the volume on the show is entirely too high when I answer Jackie's call.

"What are you guys doing?" she asks. "How'd today go?"

I tell her about our walk and the new book she's excited about. When I start talking about the arroz con pollo we had for dinner, Jackie stops me. "Wait, what are you watching?"

Fuck. I reach over to grab the remote from Mom so I can turn it down, but she pulls it just out of reach. "Turn it down," I mouth to her, but she shakes her head and turns her attention back to the drama.

"Do I hear Teresa yelling? Are you watching Housewives?"

"Uh, no," I mutter unconvincingly. "It's um–"

"What the fuck, Sam? She can't watch that shit."

I roll my eyes. "Oh come on, it's just a TV show. How dangerous could a TV show be for her? She enjoys it."

"It's not about that," she yells. "It's about reducing her overall stress. The more often she's stressed, the higher her blood pressure remains. She's already at a greater risk for a heart attack or stroke with this disease. Do you want to shorten her life even more?"

I jump to my feet and stride angrily up the stairs toward my room before responding. Mom doesn't need to hear me fighting with Jackie. Shutting the door behind me, I shout, "Are you fucking serious? You think I abandoned my career just to send Mom to an early grave?"

She sighs heavily, clearly irritated. "Sam, this was all explained in the notebook. I went into detail about the shows that get her amped up and Housewives is one of them. It's not about being petty and keeping her away from her favorite things. We're trying to ensure that her lifestyle is calm and healthy to slow the progression."

"Look, I get it," I reply, resigned and feeling a bit foolish. "I just wanted to make her happy."

"That's not the job. She's not your child. She's your mother, and she's dying. You're not responsible for keeping her spirits up; it's about keeping her alive. Marty and I have created a specific routine for her, and there's a reason for everything. You can't just show up one day and undo our hard work."

That seems harsh, but I can't come up with a counterpoint.

Jackie sighs again. "Just read the fucking notebook and follow the instructions."

I don't want to tell her I haven't read more than a few paragraphs in the notebook, but clearly, she's figured that out. She has no idea about my dyslexia, and there's no point in sharing that information now. "Okay."

"I have to give Xavier a bath," she says, rushing me off the phone. "Can you handle this?"

"Yeah," I tell her. I might've been gone a while, but I'm here now, and I don't want to mess this up. "I can handle it."

"Good."

She hangs up immediately, and I'm left feeling like even more of a failure than when I first arrived. And it's only been one day.

CHAPTER 4

MYLO

"Where is Kyan?" I ask my brothers, my patience quickly slipping away. Uncrossing my ankles and sitting up straight on the leather couch, I go through my notes again on my tablet while the rest of them chat quietly amongst themselves. Vanessa is also here and is snacking on a jar of pickles in the kitchen.

Zev looks at the digital clock above the TV and shrugs. "He said he would be here."

"These meetings are important," I remind them. "Why must I keep saying that? We skipped the last one. I will not skip another."

"We are aware of their importance, brother," Axil mutters grumpily, crossing his arms over his chest. "It is why *we* arrived on time. Save your reminders for the tardy member of this household."

Just as I let out a bone-weary sigh, the front door swings open, and in stomps Kyan, looking as frustrated as he usually does at the end of a long workday. "Apologies for my late arrival."

I shouldn't needle him, but it is impossible to resist. "Another day of big money deals at the office, brother? The sending of stern one-line emails and the ordering about of assistants?"

He huffs a breath as he toes off his dress shoes, marches into the kitchen and heads straight for the snack cabinet. After grabbing a bottle of water from the fridge, he places his nightly bag of kettle corn in the microwave. "I take pride in my work, and I have no assistants, but please," he pauses, his mouth curving into an arrogant smirk, "continue with your lazy and inaccurate accounts of what you think I do."

He is quite skilled at needling me as well, which is probably why we are always at each other's throats. "You think I don't take pride in my work?" I rise to my feet, tossing my tablet on the couch. "I do all that I can to improve the state of this town's library, yet every one of my budget requests has been denied by the council."

"Then perhaps it is time you funded the library yourself, if you truly care that much about it, and stop whining about it to those of us with bigger matters to attend to," Kyan mutters casually as he watches the bag in the microwave inflate with popped corn. Once it's done, he pours it into a large plastic bowl and makes his way to the recliner across from me.

I return to my spot, my anger boiling beneath the surface, but I swallow it, refusing to take the bait. "I have purchased hundreds of books and donated them to the library over the years. What I need are funds to improve the state of the building. That can only come from the powers that be. The newly elected councilman in charge of our district has proven to be a deeply unpleasant male. I can't pay for them myself without questions being asked about the source of my wealth. That would draw attention to our family, which we don't need."

Kyan reclines in the chair, placing the bowl on his stomach as he lets out a dramatic yawn, for which he doesn't even cover his mouth. His manners are atrocious.

"When did you become such a boorish beast?" I ask, leveling him with a look of disgust.

"When did you start using contractions like a wingless commoner?" he replies in a snarky tone.

"Contractions were seen as peasant-speak on Sufoi, but not here," I point out. "The stiffer we sound to humans, the more at risk we are for being exposed."

In response, he tosses popcorn into his mouth and chews loudly, exposing all of us to the gnashing of his teeth as they crush each popped kernel. "Can we get on with it? I require sleep, and soon."

His wretchedness is not worthy of my continued attention. I grab my tablet and swipe through the notes to the correct section. "Very well. Let us commence this meeting with our findings. Axil, what have you learned from news and documentaries about human life?"

"Police continue to abuse their power, but that is not necessarily news. Oh, and that humans detest their females," he says. "It can be the only reason for the many laws that have been unfairly shackled to their bodies."

"Mmm. Amen, my love," Vanessa mumbles from the kitchen with her mouth full of dill pickle.

"Why is she here?" Kyan asks. "I thought this meeting was exclusively for us."

Axil growls as he rises to his feet and steps toward Kyan, cracking his knuckles as he goes. He leans down next to Kyan's ear, "Do you have a problem with my mate's presence, brother?"

"Calm yourself. I am quite fond of Vanessa," he replies quickly with his hands raised in surrender. "It is merely that we were assigned different forms of media in order to study humans, and in these meetings, we share our findings. Do you not find it odd to have a human in our midst as we discuss this information?"

"On the contrary," I say, delighted to prove Kyan wrong on this point. "It's crucial to have a human we can trust to confirm our findings. Without Vanessa, we would still believe your claim from a previous meeting, the one about," I swipe back to the minutes from that meeting, "the importance of giving your mate a single rose when you decide to keep them."

Vanessa chuckles as she closes the pickle jar and washes her hands. She wipes them dry on a paper towel and joins us in the living room, stretching on her tiptoes as Axil lowers himself, so she may place a kiss on his cheek. He then gathers her in his arms and takes his seat with her on his lap. "Yeah, that's only something that happens on *The Bachelor,* fellas. Don't expect a woman to agree to become your mate just because you hand her a flower."

"So human females do not like flowers?" Axil asks, jerking back. "I thought you enjoyed the corsage I gave you."

"Oh no, we love flowers," Vanessa says, entwining her fingers with Axil's and giving his hand a reassuring squeeze. "I adored my corsage. They're just not as transactional as they are in the show. By all means, hand out beautiful bouquets of flowers to whomever you're interested in, but don't expect something in return. Women don't owe you anything."

We nod in unison at Vanessa's words.

Kyan rubs his neatly shaven, pointed chin. "Then...does that mean ninety days is not a standard window of time for humans to fall in love?"

Vanessa lets out a loud giggle, then covers her mouth, looking embarrassed as she realizes she is the only one who finds this funny. "Oh, Kyan. No, babe. It doesn't always happen in ninety days. That's just a dating show theme."

Kyan slams the recliner's footrest down with his legs and smacks his bowl onto the coffee table. "I request a new assignment," he shouts, glaring at me. "Reality TV is a lie, and I have grown tired of its deliberate trickery."

My answer comes easily and with unbridled glee. "Your request is denied."

"Outrageous!"

"Easy, brother," Zev tells him.

"Again, this is why we need Vanessa. Whatever else you learn from reality TV, confirm it with her before you accept it as truth," I instruct. "Then you will not be so easily tricked."

Zev raises his hand, and says, "May I go next? I am quite eager to discuss my findings."

I gesture for him to continue.

His eyes light up as he leans forward. "Well, I have spent much time familiarizing myself with the musical catalogs of Mozart, Prince, and The Rolling Stones—brilliant and talented humans, I must say— and I have come to a rather important realization."

"That is?" Axil asks.

"I wish to abandon my career as a tattoo artist and focus on becoming a skilled musician."

"That is...quite the realization," I reply, unsure of how to proceed with this admission. It is not as if Zev would struggle financially if he were to leave his current job. We have enough money in our coffers to support future generations, but I worry about the state of Zev's mind with a choice like this.

He has had many jobs in the sixteen years since we landed on Earth, and his overall satisfaction fades quickly with each one. He seems lost, and whenever he decides to begin a new career, he has this same palpable excitement. But how long will it last? "Are you certain you are ready for such an endeavor?"

Although, given how long draxilios live, it's likely each of us will change careers multiple times. We have all just entered our third century, putting us halfway through the average draxilio's lifespan. There is much left to learn.

"I am," he says confidently. "I have already mastered the violin and piano. Next, I would like to learn how to play the guitar."

"That makes sense, given your ability to connect with machines," Kyan notes.

"Well, I hope you do not plan on becoming famous like The Tumbling Stones, or whatever they are called," Axil adds in a stern voice. He sounds more like Luka with each passing day, though I would never tell him that. "You cannot risk it."

"I have no intention of pursuing a life of fame," Zev says, shaking his head in a way that shows how serious he is about his vow. "I do not even desire attention when I play."

He has never enjoyed the feeling of everyone's eyes on him. Zev is a sensitive, shy male with a well of emotions that runs deeper than the sea. Our handlers were cruel to him, and I have often wondered if that is why he's so withdrawn. I am starting to rethink that assumption, however.

"There will be no risk to us," Zev adds. "I merely wish to nurture this desire and create something that I find interesting and enjoyable."

"Then we support you," I tell him.

"Truly?" he asks, looking around the room.

My brothers nod as does Vanessa.

Quiet settles over the room, and I say, "I believe it's my turn to share, and I think you should settle into your seats. I have many books, TV shows, and movies I wish to discuss."

A collective groan fills the air as I launch into my very long list.

* * *

The next day, I find myself inundated with work that keeps me locked in my office. I speak with several managers of local restaurants in an effort to get them to partner with us for upcoming fundraisers. Despite the mocking tone of Kyan's suggestion last night to fund the library myself, it did inspire me to find other ways of improving my place of work.

I have held fundraisers for the library in the past, but none have accumulated more than a few hundred dollars. But a partnership with a restaurant is sure to yield better results. Especially when we offer food and drinks during trivia nights that celebrate movies and TV shows that are based on books.

We shall start with *Bridgerton* as it is extremely popular at the moment, given how quickly each book in the series flies off our shelves, and then include older favorites such as *The Hunger Games, Outlander,* and more. Entrants have the chance to win a gift card to the restaurant we partner with.

"Brilliant," I mutter quietly to myself as I create a spreadsheet to track all the details.

"Mylo?" Charlie says over the intercom. "Someone's here to see you. Her name is Sam."

Our mate, my draxilio purrs.

Not our mate, I remind him.

Pressing the button on the intercom, I reply, "Send her up."

She walks in with a stack of books so high, I can't see her face. I jump up from my chair and race around the desk to help her. Taking the books from her hands, I place them on the side table.

"Whew, thank you," she says, slightly out of breath. Her oval face glows from exertion, and it reminds me of the way she looks after we have sex, except, sadly, she is fully clothed. She's wearing a loose tank top the color of plums that is knotted at the waist, with a black lace bra peeking out from her low neckline.

I feel myself getting hard as I stare at that little scrap of fabric. Her black leggings cling to her soft curves, and I ache to peel them off her thick thighs and bite into the part of her ass that meets her thigh. The light squeak of her gold sneakers across the floor would normally bother my sensitive ears, but I am far too mesmerized by the black lace that disappears beneath her shirt. "Those are the overdue books my mom had. Sorry again about that."

"You did not have to carry those up here," I tell her, gesturing for her to take the seat across from me. "You could've left them in the return box outside."

Her expression is unreadable, but once she is seated, I detect a hint of shyness in the way her hands are folded in her lap and her inability to meet my gaze. "I know, but I wanted to make sure you knew all were accounted for."

"I thank you for that."

She scratches her head, looking distinctly uncomfortable. "That woman at the front desk. I think I saw her here yesterday."

"Ah, yes, that is Charlie. Today is her first day as assistant librarian."

Samantha nods as she nibbles on her bottom lip. "She's very pretty."

"I guess," I reply. I suppose Charlie does have nice curves and a pleasing smile, though her beauty is not something I paid much attention to as she is not a female I am trying to woo, but rather a qualified candidate for a position I have been trying to fill for months.

Something about Charlie's presence clearly bothers Samantha, though I cannot figure out why. She's not jealous, is she? No, that cannot be it. She has made it clear there are no feelings between the two of us, so I ignore that theory and change the subject. "What are your plans for the day? Is your mother here?"

"No, she's home. I told her not to move from her chair in the living room until I got back," she says with a half-smile. Then her brown eyes go unfocused as she stares at the corner of my desk. "I feel like I need to watch every breath she takes. It's a lot more intense than I thought it would be."

"Caring for your mother, you mean?"

Samantha lets out a deep whoosh of breath. "Yeah."

I wish to comfort her because it is clear she needs comforting, but I am surprised she came to me for it. I'm not sure how to proceed. "Do you...wish to talk about it?"

My words seem to break through her thoughts as she shakes her head and puts on a smile that I can tell is not genuine.

"Nah, it's fine. Don't worry about it," she says, straightening her spine. "I think I'm still getting used to my new life." Leaning forward, she places her elbows on the edge of the desk and rests her face in her hands. She lets out an excited gasp at the sight of my bowl of Starburst. "Where are the yellow ones?" she asks as grabs several reds and pinks in her fist.

"The yellow ones are my favorite. I've eaten them all."

"You don't like the pink ones?"

"No," I reply. "I should take these home for my brothers. They enjoy the other flavors."

She narrows her gaze at me as she chews. "You know you can buy the individual colors in bulk, right?"

"What? You can?"

"Yeah," she says with an amused laugh. "On Amazon. I'll send you the link." She finishes the candies and gestures toward my hands. "Gimme."

Confused, but more curious, I do as she says. Samantha uncurls her fist and drops several pink and red Starburst wrappers into my palm. "Buy yourself something nice," she says with a smirk.

It's such an odd thing to do; I'm unsure of how to respond. "Um, you realize this is not an acceptable form of currency."

She makes a "psh" sound with her mouth. "Not with that attitude."

She brushes a stray curl off her forehead and asks, "What are you up to today?"

"I am putting together a rather marvelous fundraiser," I state proudly, my chest puffing a bit at my hard work. "Next month, we will hold a trivia night with a *Bridgerton* theme. The food and drinks will be donated by Supreme Buns—lemonade and finger sandwiches. Is that not perfect? And there will be prizes."

"Wow, that sounds amazing," she says, impressed. "I think people will love that." She chews on the inside of her cheek for a moment. "Do you need any help? Organizing with the vendor or social media promotion?"

"Oh, no, Samantha," I tell her. It is nice of her to offer, but she has far too much to occupy her time as it is. "You don't need to do anything. I can enlist Charlie for help."

Her face falls. "Right. Charlie."

"But I would love it if you attended the event," I offer in an attempt to lift her expression into one of joy. "Perhaps you will be the winner of the night."

"Probably not, actually. I've never read the books or watched the show."

I jerk back in my seat, unable to believe the words that just left her pretty mouth. "You are not serious."

She laughs. "Dead serious."

"Do you not enjoy historical romance?"

"Mmm, I'm not a fan of romance in general, actually."

Now I am utterly speechless. Based on the borrowing data, it is clear that human females enjoy reading the romance genre more than males, and I shall never understand this because the genre serves as a clear guide for what females are seeking from their partners.

Why would the males of this planet waste such an opportunity to give them what they desire? But setting aside male foolishness for a moment, what Samantha says simply does not compute. It is obvious she does not enjoy the act of reading in the traditional sense, but she does not even enjoy listening to romance on audiobook?

"Why not?" I finally ask.

She shrugs. "I don't know. It just seems kind of trite, I guess."

"What does?"

"You know, love. Eternal happiness with the same person. It just… it's a nice idea, I just don't really get it."

I try to process this. "You do not get it."

Samantha sighs and rubs her palms against her black leggings. "My dad left us when I was three. I don't even remember him. And my mom never dated anyone else, so I didn't exactly have a prime example of a healthy relationship to look up to. I, uh, I grew up, got married because I thought I was in love, but it faded quickly, and now, I don't know. I guess I see it as something I need proof of to believe in, you know?"

"You are close with Vanessa, though, and you must be able to see how in love she and Axil are."

"Oh yeah, I've seen other people fall in love," she replies, then grows quiet as she focuses intently on her fingertips. "But it doesn't happen for everyone."

I open my mouth to respond to the words she did not say—that even though she clearly does not believe love was meant to find her, it will, but she holds up both hands, stopping me. "Don't move."

"Uh," I begin.

"Nope, don't look at me," she instructs while pulling her phone out of the purse at her feet. "Hold your face right where it is and tilt your chin just a little bit to the left."

Seconds feel like hours as I hold myself still. Now that Sam has told me not to look her way, it is the only thing I want to do.

"Okay, got it," she eventually says, beaming as she swipes across her screen. "Sorry, the sun was hitting your shoulders and cheekbones perfectly."

"May I see?"

She walks around my desk and leans over my shoulder to show me, her long curls brushing against my cheek. Her hair smells of peppermint, and the perfume she applied to the pulse point on her neck has faded but is still present. Warm. Intoxicating.

"See the way the light pours in all around you like it's wrapping you in a hug? Incredible, right?" she asks.

"Incredible," I repeat in a hoarse voice, my throat suddenly dry. I'm not looking at the pictures, or even in the direction of her phone. My eyes are locked on the end of one of her perfect curls, my fingers twitching with desperation to touch it. "Yes, truly."

"*Ours. Ours. Ours,*" my draxilio chants inside my head.

She straightens and grabs her bag off the floor. "Care if I post it?"

"Uh, no," I reply, still in a daze from her closeness.

"I have to get back home, but I'll see you tonight?"

"Yes," I tell her. "I shall arrive at eight to read to your mother."

She shoots me a smile before the door closes behind her, and it takes several minutes for me to return to reality.

Suddenly, tonight cannot come soon enough.

CHAPTER 5

SAM

*I*t's pouring rain when Mylo arrives, with thunder cracking through the sky, causing our too-thin windows to vibrate. Yet he still shows up five minutes early. I thought he looked hot in his true form, but *dios mío*, wet Mylo is also a tasty snack.

Droplets cling to the ends of his dirty blond hair, and as he removes his raincoat and kicks off his shoes, I watch a drop land on his forehead and travel down the side of his face, over the sharpened edge of his cheekbone, and disappear into the dimple next to his mouth. I find myself, for the first time ever, envious of a tiny drop of water.

"Here," I say, handing him a towel.

He runs it roughly through his hair, then carefully wipes his glasses clean. "Do I look ridiculous?" he asks, his face scrunching up as he surveys the dampness of his clothes.

"Not at all," I tell him honestly. "You look like a guy who weathered a storm just to read a bedtime story to an old lady."

"Who are you calling old, Papita?" Mom hollers from her bedroom upstairs.

Mylo laughs heartily as he climbs the steps and walks ahead of me down the hall, his grin widening when he finds her room. "Good evening, Elena," he greets her with a bow. Then turns to me. "You are Papita, I gather?"

"No, we don't need to get into–" I start to say, but Mom pats a spot at the foot of the bed and launches into the story.

"When Sammy was little, she got tired of playing with dolls and became obsessed with Mr. Potato Head. She wanted an entire army of Mr. Potato Heads, but I was working two jobs at the time and couldn't afford to get her more, so one night I handed her a russet potato that I had drawn a smiley face on."

I climb into bed next to Mom, over the covers, and she grabs my hand. My cheeks are bright red, I can feel them, but there's no getting out of this.

"So a week goes by, and I notice the bowl of potatoes in the kitchen suddenly has only two left."

I'd be annoyed with the fact that she's sharing this embarrassing story if it weren't for how much fun she's having. Her face is lit up as she giggles and elbows me in the ribs to make sure I'm paying attention. I don't love the nickname, and I've always assumed it had a double meaning relating to my size, but it's hard to be mad at her when she's reliving a memory in detail. I'm grateful this moment exists at all.

"I go up to her room, and through the door I can hear her talking, just chatting away," she continues. "When I open it a crack, she's surrounded by a dozen potatoes. They're covered in marker scribbles and wearing doll hats and other accessories. She's talking to each one as if they're her best friends." She's laughing so hard at this point that she wipes the tears from her eyes and leans her head on my shoulder. "Hence, my little 'Ita."

Mylo's smile reaches his eyes as he continues to laugh. "Potato friends are almost as good as real friends."

She turns to look at me. "I think you gave them all names and birthdays, too, didn't you?"

"I did," I say, rubbing my forehead. "I only remember Tag and Bianca, though. They were my Barbie and Ken."

"Oh, Bianca!" my mom shouts excitedly. "Was Bianca the one you snuck into school with you?"

Ugh, I forgot about that. This is getting painful now. "I believe so, yeah."

Mom is practically bouncing as she continues. "I got a call at work one day from her teacher asking why Sammy has a rotten potato in her desk."

"You let your potato friends rot?" he asks me with mock sincerity. "How sad."

"Well, my other dolls didn't do that, and throwing a friend in the trash seemed cruel, so…" I trail off.

"I had to buy her a brand-new bag of them that night," Mom adds. "And she sobbed as I threw each rancid potato in the garbage." Mom looks at me with eyes full of unshed tears. "Such a fiercely independent girl. Never caring what others think." She presses a kiss to the back of my hand. "*Mi cielo.*"

Mylo's brow furrows in a way that makes him look amused by the tale. "Did you keep the same names for the new potatoes?"

"No, they weren't the same potatoes, so why would I give them the same names?"

He nods as he leans back and rests his elbow on the bed's wooden footboard, putting his veiny, muscular forearm on display. My cheeks grow hot just looking at it. "Excellent point."

Mylo grabs *Wed to the Alien Warlord* by January Bell off my mother's nightstand and begins to read. Time flies as he reads the first seven chapters, his voice smooth and animated as he goes, getting into character just enough to keep me fully engaged, but not overdoing it by attempting a woman's voice when the point of view switches between the lead characters with each chapter.

At one point, I look at Mom and find her eyes locked on Mylo, a warm smile tugging at her lips, and I realize what an incredible gift he has given me. I focus on her face as I file this moment away in my brain. I need to remember it later. When the next bad day comes and she can't remember me and she's frustrated and scared of what awaits her, I'll think of this.

It's a little past nine when she drifts off to the sound of Mylo's voice, and he and I exchange a nod to leave and let her sleep. I press a kiss to her forehead, pull up the blankets beneath her chin, and turn off the light on her nightstand before closing the door to her room.

Once Mylo and I are alone, I decide to show him just how thankful I am. I tug on his hand and pull him down the hall to my room, locking the door behind us once we're inside.

"Wha–" he starts, but I silence him with a kiss.

I love that I keep catching him off guard with my boldness. Then I remember a question I still haven't gotten an answer to and pull back. "Mylo, why did you offer to read to Mom?"

One side of his mouth curves up into a half-grin. "I have seen many children read at the library during the monthly practice session I offer for students who are struggling with reading comprehension. The look on your face when she asked you to read to her is one I have seen before."

I nod, saying nothing and waiting for him to continue.

"I would guess that you have the brain condition that jumbles the letters in front of you." Nervously, he searches my face. "Am I right?"

The sigh I let out is so heavy, I feel like I'd float away if Mylo's arms weren't holding me in place. "Yes," I whisper, the admission instantly removing decades of stress and anxiety that have kept my back muscles tightly knotted.

"It is quite common, you know," he says, crooking a finger under my chin, forcing me to look deep into his eyes. He holds me tighter, and I melt into his embrace. "Many people struggle with it."

I know this, of course, but it's nice to be reminded. I've spent many hours listening to audiobooks on the subject, but on the spot, when I'm asked to read something and I know I won't be able to, it's isolating. I feel stupid and embarrassed. That's why not many people in my life know about it. And Nate only found out because I told him.

Mylo, on the other hand, spotted it right away, and saved me from having to disappoint my mother. Walking him backward, I nudge him down to a seated position on the edge of my bed. His mouth falls open when I drop to my knees.

"Samantha, you do not have to," he says with a ragged sigh.

"I want to," I reassure him, reaching for the waist of his pants. He lifts his hips as I tug on his pants and boxer briefs, pulling them down to his ankles. I free one of his feet and spread his thighs, so I can settle in between them.

He's naked from the waist down, looking inhumanly large on my tiny bed. Then I remember, he's not human, and that's how I prefer him.

"Unmask for me," I say, wrapping my hand around his cock. It fills my hand to the point that my fingers don't touch. I can't believe this man is all mine.

The moment the thought settles in my mind, I picture Charlie's face, and remember that, no, he's not all mine. And it's not Charlie I'm jealous of, specifically. It's what she represents: all the beautiful women who enter Mylo's life, and are, I'm sure, completely smitten with him. Who wouldn't be? He's a hot nerd who gives more than he takes, and he has the body every male Avenger aspires to.

We never agreed to be exclusive. In fact, I was the one who said "never again" the last time we hooked up. Yet, here I am, about to gobble his cock like it's an ice cream cone. Clearly, I can't keep myself away. Maybe I should stop trying.

My eyes widen when his shaft turns a darker shade of blue than the rest of him, and I gasp when his ridges emerge, tickling the inside of my palm. "Sorry, still not totally used to that," I say with a chuckle as I re-tighten my grip. He's hard and hot and swollen in my hand, and my throat dries up like the Sahara.

He props himself up on his elbows and shoots me an amused grin. "Take your time."

Saliva fills my mouth as I slowly stroke down the length of him and back up. "Nah," I mutter before taking him deep into my throat. I gag slightly about halfway down, and silently curse that I can't take more of him. This isn't the first time I've given him head—I slobbered all over this snake the first night we were together—so his size isn't what shocks me; it's more the way the ridges fill my cheeks. But I do my best to hollow them as I suck.

Mylo's long, thick fingers lace into my hair, holding my head in place. His hold isn't painful, but forceful. Just the way I like it. "Yes, Samantha," he groans, and the throaty way he says my full name has the walls of my pussy contracting.

I release him in order to focus my tongue on the bulbous head of his cock, swirling around it and licking the drop of precome that pools at the tip. It's hot as it slides down my throat, and I moan at the spicy, salty taste of him.

"You like my come, don't you?" Mylo says, his voice husky and arrogant as I take him deep once again. "You want me to fuck that pretty mouth?"

"Mmm," I mutter, my mouth completely filled. I love when he talks to me like this. It's the opposite of the controlled, polite bookworm he is with everyone else. When we're together like this, he's a crass, wild animal.

His grip tightens in my hair, and I hold still as he thrusts into my mouth. I hold onto him, my fingernails digging into his tight, bare ass as he fucks my face, my eyes watering as I gag on the sheer size of him.

He lets out a breathy hiss as his hips buck, faster and harder, until the thrusts take on an erratic edge. "*Fuck.* Your mouth is so fucking hot."

Moments later, his grip loosens as he chases his release; a never-ending stream of hot come spurts into my mouth and down my throat. I swallow all I can, loving it and thirsty for more, but it's too much. His come dribbles past my lips and down my chin until he's fully sated. Instinct tells me to wipe it off, but I end up leaving it, if only to see his reaction when he notices it. Once his breaths even out, he sits up and his gaze lands on my chin.

His gray eyes swirl with heat as he takes his thumb and gathers the seed from my mouth and chin and pushes that thumb between my lips. "I like seeing my mark on you."

I swallow the rest and lightly nip on the pad of his thumb.

"My draxilio likes it even more."

"Oh yeah? I didn't realize I was making your dragon happy too," I tell him, preening a bit at his praise. "But honestly, it wasn't a chore. I love sucking you off."

His big hand wraps around the back of my neck and pulls me to him in a hungry, bruising kiss. I'm breathless when he pulls away, and when his lips brush lightly against the tip of my nose, I melt.

Eventually, we separate and I check my phone as Mylo gets dressed, going from one app to the next and scrolling mindlessly. When I get to Instagram, little red hearts and conversation bubbles fill the top of the screen, and I'm briefly confused until I check the photo of Mylo I posted a few hours ago. "Holy shit," I mutter as I scroll through the responses.

My account has a decent following, but none of my photos have ever gone viral. Mylo has changed that.

"What is it?" he asks, coming to look over my shoulder. Hot breath fans my neck as I show him the post. "All this for a photo of…me?"

"Yeah, you sexy dweeb," I tell him. He can't possibly be surprised by his own beauty, can he? "I mentioned the library and the fundraiser in the comments, but you need to capitalize on this."

"What do you suggest?"

"Well, the library doesn't have an account. I checked before I posted this. So set one up immediately and make sure you're the face of it."

"Me? Really?"

"Yes!" I quietly shout, so as not to wake my mom. "No one is engaging with this photo because of the blurry stack of books in the corner, Mylo."

He chuckles and slowly returns to his pale, hornless mask. "Okay, I will do that as soon as I get home."

I turn to face him, and he pulls me in for another toe-curling kiss, then whispers against my lips, "Never again, Sidney?" using the fake name I gave him the night we met.

"Correct, Marco. Never again," I say back. It's a lie. We both know it, but now it's also a fun little game, and I love games.

CHAPTER 6

SAM

*W*eeks pass in a blink, and Mylo and I get into a routine of doing it and promising we never will again. We almost get caught more than once by either Zev or Kyan roaming around the house late at night, but luckily Axil and Vanessa are mostly at her house, and it doesn't seem like they have any inkling of what's going on.

I'm most worried about Vanessa finding out because then she'll want to play matchmaker so that both of us can live happily ever after with our dragon mates, and getting married a second time is not something I want.

Mylo reads to Mom once a week and stays after she falls asleep so we can fool around quietly in my room. It's like high school, except the sex I have in my room now lasts longer than five minutes, and it's actually good. We end up in my room or his every night of the week, and he's insisted on reading romance novels to me after sex, which I always fall asleep to, but I find I am enjoying the genre more than I thought I would. We've finished *Red, White, and Royal Blue*, *The Kiss Quotient*, and *Shanna*, already.

Without a normal work schedule, I lose track of the days. It's only when I get a text from Marty reminding me that we're having family dinner here tonight that I realize it's been a month since I came home.

And since I've been home, today is the worst day I've had with Mom yet. The morning started off terrible and has stayed terrible. She went outside and started wandering while I was in the shower, and I didn't know she had gotten lost until I was running around the house in sweats, a sports bra, and a towel wrapped around my hair screaming her name because I couldn't find her. I lost the towel between the stairs and the car and drove with sopping-wet hair down the neighboring streets until I found her barefoot at the bus stop.

She didn't recognize me when I pulled up, so it took some convincing to get her into the car, but eventually, she was too cold in just her nightgown to stay put. I got her home, showered, and fed, but she fought me every step of the way, refusing to do whatever I asked, and accusing me of manipulating her so I could steal her jewelry.

She loves the telenovela *La Casa de las Flores*, so in an effort to give myself a break, I put on old episodes in the living room for her while I cleaned our bedrooms.

As I'm changing her sheets, I discover a pile of used tissues beneath her pillows. There must be a hundred of them, balled up and sticking together. It's bizarre. "What the hell?" I march downstairs to the living room with a wad of them in my hand. "Mom, what is this? Why are all these tissues under your pillow?"

She stares blankly at me. "I don't know. You probably put them there to make me look bad." Then she gets to her feet on shaky legs and wags a finger at me. "What are you doing in my bedroom anyway? You think I won't notice if my rings are missing?"

The lack of logic in her response keeps my anger from rising to the surface.

"I'm onto you, girl."

She's not in her right mind. She's not in her right mind. It's a thing I've started telling myself when she gets mean.

"Fine," I mutter, returning to her bedroom and shoving the tissues into a trash bag. Once the sheets are changed, I go into my room and close the door to call Jackie.

"Hey, what's going on?" she asks nervously upon answering.

"Mom's having a bad day. I'm not sure we should do family dinner tonight."

She pulls the phone away to say something to her husband, Dan, that I can't decipher. "We can't wait for her to have a good day to reschedule. Good day or bad, we need to be there. It'll be fine."

Well, I tried. They've been warned. "Okay."

"Dan has to take the boys to William's baseball game, so it'll just be me tonight, but I think Marty is bringing Holly and the kids."

"Oh, good," I say sarcastically. "Can't wait for Holly to try convincing us celery water is the cure for Alzheimer's." She's a sweet woman, and she makes Marty happy, but her white-lady-wellness gimmicks really get under my skin. It's one thing to follow trendy diets, but to suggest others join you? Not cool.

Jackie cackles into the phone. "Or…wait, what was it last time? Drinking bone broth after fasting all day?"

"Yep," I reply, laughing too.

"Oh, and don't forget about the vagina crystals," Jackie adds.

"What's a vagina?" I hear little Xavier ask in the background.

She pulls the phone away again to speak to Xavier. "A body part that should always be respected. I'll tell you more about it another time. Now, go finish your carrot sticks, okay?"

"Hey," I say, lowering my voice just in case Mom is listening at the bottom of the stairs, "I found a bunch of used tissues under Mom's pillow. Is this something you've dealt with? I don't know what to do."

"Ah," she says knowingly. "She's hoarding again. Yeah, I found loose cashews in her sock drawer a couple times."

"Loose cashews?"

"It happens," she says calmly. "Dr. Fisher said it's common for people with Alzheimer's to hoard things. I think she gets confused and assumes she won't be able to find something again or that it's about to run out, so she takes the last of it and puts it in a secret spot."

"Okay, that makes sense. Should I let it continue?"

"I would check around the room to see if she's hoarding anything else," she suggests. "Tissues seem relatively harmless. If you've already thrown them out, fine. But wait until she's in a place where you can have a rational conversation with her about it. If it's food, take care of it immediately so you don't end up with ants or mice, and let her know that's why she can't hoard stuff anymore. It's not about taking away her stuff, it's about preventing pests."

"Yeah, okay. I'll check the rest of her room." I let out a relieved sigh at the reminder that I'm not in this alone.

"Okay, I need to help Xavier with his homework before the game. I'll see you in a few hours."

"Okay, bye."

As soon as I hang up the phone, it starts to ring, and Mylo's viral photo flashes across my screen. "How's the sexiest man in Sudbury?"

He chuckles, the sound low and throaty, and it sends goose bumps across my skin. "The library has one hundred thousand followers now."

"The library? *You* have a hundred thousand followers, which is way more than I have at this point. Took me years to grow my photography account, and it took you a month to surpass me. You're welcome, by the way."

He clears his throat and lowers his voice to a whisper. "I believe I thanked you last night. Twice."

Mmm. He did indeed. I'm pretty sure I blacked out at the tail end of that second orgasm. "You have one talented tongue, sir."

"I'd be honored to thank you again tonight…"

Since this is day one of my period, going down on me is a no-go, but we can get creative. "I want to, but I have dinner with the family tonight. I'm not sure how late it'll go, but I'll text you when we're done."

"Can't wait," he replies.

I can't either. For so many reasons.

I spend the next hour going through every nook and cranny of Mom's room. There were a dozen loose cashews in her sock drawer, but that wasn't nearly as shocking as the open can of beans and the unfinished container of cottage cheese in the back corner of her closet, covered in a colony of ants that were marching their way toward a crack in the wall.

"Fó," I mutter to myself, goose bumps covering my skin at the sight. Bile rises in my throat, and I have to hold my breath as I clear Mom's old sneakers from around the pile of pungent rot. She's distracted enough by her show to not notice when I race down the stairs and grab the Raid, a pair of dishwashing gloves, and several plastic grocery bags from under the kitchen sink and run back up to her room.

Once I've got the gloves on, I hold my breath again and blast the two open containers with a steady spray until most of the ants appear to be dead in a pool of chemicals, then I use the plastic bags as another barrier between my skin and this disgusting mess and grab the bean and cheese mush and race to dump the contents on the patio. A tall glass of water is all takes to rinse away the ant-filled containers, and the bottle of Raid runs dry after I spray what's left into the crack in the wall, praying to Jesus that I've defeated the remaining members of the ant colony.

I don't find anything else in Mom's room, but after what I discovered, I'm not sure it could get much worse, and at least now I know to keep an eye on the ant situation.

By the time Marty and Jackie arrive for dinner, Mom's mood has gone from angry to apathetic, which, after today, I'm fine with. She's not herself, but she's not hurling accusations at me either.

"I didn't have the energy to cook, so I ordered a bunch of Chinese food," I say as I greet Marty and Holly, gesturing toward the white boxes covering the dining room table. Then I wrap their kids, Oliver and Penny, in bear hugs and cover their cheeks with smacking kisses until they're each giggling and saying "Auntie Sam!" in mock embarrassment.

I also make a point to show Jackie the containers of steamed vegetables for Mom so she doesn't scold me too much.

Jackie hands Holly a plate, but she declines. "I'm doing a detox cleanse right now. It's supposed to be great for your kidneys. I can send you the article if you want your mom to try it."

I grit my teeth in an effort to keep my eyes from rolling. *Don't take the bait*, I tell myself. But a moment later, the question falls out of my mouth. "Isn't that what your kidneys do already? Detox and cleanse. I'm pretty sure that's their whole purpose."

"I know, right?" Holly says, oblivious to my tone. "The cleanse makes them even more efficient."

Jackie and I exchange looks that are an equal combination of bewilderment and exasperation, but we both refrain from further comments. It's not worth it.

Marty is loading his plate with chicken fried rice when he points to a square piece of paper on the side table where we keep the mail. "Oh, Sam, I brought over your invitation to Nate's wedding. I kept forgetting to bring it. Sorry about that."

"Oh," I mutter, grabbing the paper and examining it closely. I stare at the name of my ex-husband, smushed so closely to this unknown woman's name, who is apparently his bride-to-be. "I didn't realize Nate was engaged."

"Seriously?" Marty asks, his face scrunching in surprise.

"Yeah, I haven't talked to him in, like," I search my mind, trying to remember, "eight months. He texted me on my birthday, but that was it."

"Wow, Nate's getting married?" Jackie asks. "Good for him."

"Yeah, good for him," I agree. I want him to be happy. He deserves happiness. "I just don't understand why I was invited."

"That is weird," Jackie adds. "Maybe he just wants you to see how well he's doing, you know? He wants the upper hand."

"The upper hand for what?" I ask. "We're divorced."

"Or maybe they have a minimum they need to hit for the venue, and they just need bodies," Jackie offers.

"But out of everyone they could invite, shouldn't I be dead last?"

"I thought you guys were good friends," Marty says, taking a seat between Holly and Oliver. "We grabbed a beer last month, and he told me you were."

It's odd that my brother hangs out with my ex, but even still, I have no idea why Nate would lie about the two of us being anything more than cordial acquaintances. I guess it doesn't matter. "We're not. Are you going?"

"Yep," Marty replies, taking a sip of his beer. "I need to let him know that my RSVP is wrong, though, because I included Holly, but she's decided to stay home with the kids."

"Going solo then, eh? Have fun," I tell him.

"No, you're coming with me," he replies, looking at me expectantly.

I stop chewing my lo mein and stare at him, puzzled by his words.

"I sent back our RSVPs at the same time, and I marked that you were coming."

The lo mein feels like a ball of sludge as I swallow it down. My body moves of its own accord, bristling with rage as I get to my feet and plant my fists on either side of my plate. "Why the fuck would you do that?"

Holly holds up a hand and starts speaking to me like I'm a terrorist holding a bomb. "Sam, we're really trying to avoid outward displays of anger or swearing in front of the kids, so—"

"Then maybe the kids should play outside for a bit," I say through gritted teeth, still staring daggers at my brother.

"Play outside?" Holly asks, aghast, as she looks out the sliding glass doors to the patio. "It's dark out."

If I had any shred of patience left in me, I'd tell her that Mom had us playing outside well past dark countless times just to rid us of our energy before bed, and we were just fine. But I'm too focused on the fact that I'm attending my ex-husband's wedding to get into that right now.

Marty shrugs. "It's not a big deal. The invitation showed up here a few months ago, and I wasn't sure when you'd be home again…but I knew it would be before the wedding, and I figured you'd want to go, so…"

In what world would anyone want to attend their ex-spouse's wedding? Has he lost his fucking mind?

"What if they trip and hurt themselves?" Holly asks.

There goes my last nerve. "Then give them a fucking flashlight!" I shout.

Holly's scowl deepens as she dramatically reaches over and covers Penny's ears.

Jackie's mouth hangs open, but there's amusement in her eyes at the scene I'm causing. Mom sneaks a fork full of fried rice off Jackie's plate without her noticing.

Marty rises to his feet and puts his fists on the table, mirroring me, the table now creaking under our weight. "Don't yell at her. This is not my fault. I thought you were good friends, so I figured you wouldn't want to miss his big day. Get over it."

"Get over it? Really?" This is the last thing I need right now. My chest heaves when I ask, "When is the wedding?"

Marty sighs. "In two weeks."

A steady throb begins between my eyes, and I pinch the skin there, trying to make it go away. "So, just to recap, you took a wedding invitation that was addressed to me—a wedding that happens to be my ex-husband's—you opened it, RSVP'd yes on my behalf, and sent it back. And you think you were doing me a favor?"

Holly's hands drop from the sides of Penny's face, and she looks at Marty disapprovingly. "Honey, you didn't." Glad she's finally listening.

"See, even she thinks it's fucked."

Holly mouths "language" at me, and it takes all my willpower not to fling a handful of lo mein at her.

Marty sits back down and stabs the broccoli on his plate. "I don't know what else to tell you. I thought you were friends."

Eventually, I calm down enough to take my seat. "Next time, let me handle my own mail, okay?"

"Fine."

"It's pretty last-minute, but I'm sure you can tell him your plans have changed, and you can no longer attend," Jackie suggests.

It's definitely last minute with the wedding two weeks away, but I can't imagine actually going. Nate and I might be on somewhat friendly terms, but I haven't seen his family since long before the divorce, and his mom and sister are not fans of mine. They never were. They blamed me for everything that went wrong in our marriage, and the moment I filed the papers, they turned ice cold.

I also received some pretty nasty emails from them, telling me what a mistake I was making and "what kind of woman would put her career above her husband?" I'd rather take a piece of sandpaper to my clit than have to make small talk with them over bacon-wrapped shrimp and cheap champagne. "Yeah, I'll text him tomorrow or something."

"You'll still need to get him a gift," Mom notes, unhelpfully.

"Thanks, Mom," I say with a sigh.

The rest of dinner passes without incident, and Mom is delighted when Jackie lets her eat a fortune cookie. Marty and Holly take the kids home, with him muttering an apology under his breath before he leaves, which I appreciate.

I help Mom climb the stairs to the bathroom, her grip tight and her legs shakier than usual. When I come back down to clean up the dishes, Jackie pulls me aside.

"Hey, take tonight off," she says quietly. "I got this."

My heart leaps at the thought of getting a jump-start on my weekend off, but I need to make sure Jackie isn't messing with me. "Are you sure?"

She nods. "This isn't a sprint, it's a marathon. I can't have you burning out. Marty and I need you to keep being her primary caregiver. And I can tell today was…a lot. So, go out. Blow off some steam. I've already let Dan know I'm staying over tonight."

I bite my lip to hold back tears as I pull her into a smothering hug. "Thank you, thank you, thank you."

She chuckles. "You're welcome. Now get outta here."

I race into my room to change, and once I reapply my perfume, I text Mylo to let him know I'm on my way over.

He sneaks me through the side door, as usual, but when we reach the top of the stairs, I hear footsteps heading toward us.

"Mylo, have you seen my new guitar pick?" Zev asks from down the hall. Mylo holds up a hand, telling me to stay right where I am on the steps behind him. I hold my breath in an effort to remain as still and silent as possible. Intense cramps have me clutching my stomach, but I resist the urge to double over with a loud groan.

"No, I have not seen it," Mylo tells him. "Maybe it's in Axil's room."

Smart suggestion on his part since Axil's room is on the first floor and away from us. Zev's footsteps retreat, and when the coast is clear, Mylo gestures for me to follow.

"That was close," I say with a sigh once the lock on Mylo's bedroom door clicks into place.

"Indeed," he mutters as he pulls me against his hard body.

His hands are quick as they tug my shirt and bra off, but when he reaches for my pants, I stop him. He needs a warning before my high-waisted period panties are revealed. "It's day one of my period, so my downstairs is closed tonight."

His brow furrows as he looks down at my crotch, then back up to my face. "I don't understand. You don't want to have sex?"

I do, but the desire to curl into the fetal position is much stronger than my sex drive. Anger during dinner earlier kept the PMS-related discomfort at bay, but now it feels like my ovaries are being flattened in a panini press. "It's not that," I explain, "I'm not feeling great at the moment."

His eyes widen in concern as his hands land on my shoulders. "What is it? What can I do?"

"Oh, nothing," I say with a shrug. "I'm just crampy and not feeling sexy right now. It'll pass. But maybe tonight I can give you head, or–"

"No, Samantha," he interrupts. "If you are not feeling well, I don't want you sucking my cock."

I'm about to assure him it's not a big deal, and that I love giving him head, when he pulls his phone out of his pocket and starts typing. "Mylo, really, it's fine."

He ignores me as his gaze drifts over the screen of his phone, and a minute later, he goes to his closet and pulls out a pair of black sweats and a red t-shirt. "Put these on," he says, shoving them into my hands. "I shall be right back."

I'm so confused. "Wait, what?"

Mylo presses his ear against his bedroom door, listening for anyone in the hallway. Then he whispers, "Change your clothes, lie down, and I shall return shortly."

He closes the door behind him before I can say another word.

What the hell just happened? And where did he go? I'm tempted to sneak out and head back home, but the sweats in my hands are as soft as butter, and his giant bed looks so comfortable. I'll just put these on and lie down for a few minutes. Then I'll text him to see what the fuck is going on.

His t-shirt is plain, not a logo in sight, but the fabric feels soft and stretchy and incredibly well-made. I want to live in this shirt. It's so big, the bottom hem hits my knees, and I have to roll the bottom cuffs of the sweatpants four times just to keep them from dragging on the ground.

The moment I snuggle beneath his thick, downy comforter, Mylo bursts into the room with a plastic bag in his hand.

"Where'd you go?" I ask, hauling myself up into a seated position.

He empties the contents of the bag on the bed and says, "I looked up how to care for a woman on her period, and this is what the internet told me to get."

In the pile of items in front of me, there are pads, tampons, a heating pad, a bottle of Ibuprofen, a red velvet cupcake, four Milky Way bars, and a pint of chocolate chip ice cream with a plastic spoon taped to the side.

Mylo's gaze bores into mine as he waits for my reaction. "Did I miss something?" he asks nervously.

"No," I say with a surprised chuckle. It took him all of thirty seconds to register my pain, Google a solution, and go out and buy everything I could possibly want to get me through my period. "I...I can't believe you did this." I'm amused and perplexed and in awe of this man. I've never known anyone like him, and I'm starting to think I never will.

His teeth gleam as he shoots me a proud grin. "It is my pleasure, Samantha." Then he steps into his walk-in closet and changes into sweats before grabbing the heating pad from the pile. "Let me get this ready for you," before heading downstairs.

When he returns, he's holding my heating pad in one hand, and a bowl of popcorn in the other. "This is for you," he says, handing me the purple rubber bottle, "and this," he pops a piece into his mouth, "is for me."

We settle in next to each other on the bed as we dig into our snacks, and I can't stop smiling with each bite. After the shitty day I had, this is exactly what I needed, and Mylo gave it to me without hesitation. Nate never did anything like this for me. No one I've dated has. He might be the most thoughtful sex friend I've ever had.

"Would you like to watch something?" he asks. "A movie?"

I take another bite of ice cream, noticing the pint is almost half empty, and put it on the nightstand. "Actually, would you mind reading to me?" I ask, unwrapping a Milky Way and adjusting the heating pad on my stomach as I lean against his side.

His strong jaw drops open, and his eyes sparkle with delight at my request. "You want me to read to you? That will make you feel better?"

I give his hard chest a playful push. "Don't look so surprised. I love when you read to me."

He pulls his tablet off the nightstand and starts listing titles. When he mentions a book of Italian poetry, I become very intrigued. "You can speak Italian?"

"I can speak many languages," he says. "We didn't know where on Earth we would settle, so I wanted to be prepared." Then I notice him shaking his head. "I assigned certain languages to my brothers, but none of them followed my orders."

"They're not as smart or driven as you," I note, offering him a bite of my candy bar. He takes it, and his eyes widen as he chews, making him look much younger than a three-hundred-year-old dragon.

When I finish the candy, I turn on my side and rest my cheek on

Mylo's chest. He starts with a poem called *La Vita Nuova* by Dante Alighieri, and even though I can only understand a handful of words, the way he enunciates with a perfect Italian accent makes my stomach flutter. I wish I could watch the roll of his magnificent tongue when he says certain words, and that thought creates all kinds of tongue-related fantasies as he starts reading the next poem, a sonnet by Petrarch.

My mind wanders as he rubs my back and I envision us years into the future, just like this—not having sex, but caring for each other in the most intimate ways, and I'm surprised by how much joy that image brings me. His touch feels…right. As if my body has been waiting for it. Craving it.

A shudder rips through me when I consider these are not thoughts a person has about a casual sex friend. These thoughts are more. These feelings…

"Are you cold?" he whispers, breaking through my thoughts.

"No," I tell him, settling into the crook of his arm for another poem.

Eventually, I change back into my clothes and give him a kiss goodnight at the side door, then stumble home on legs that feel like jelly. I'm so distracted by thoughts of him and the way he cared for me that I don't even realize I've made it home until I'm standing in the middle of my bedroom. The moment my head hits the pillow, I pass out, more satisfied than I thought possible, considering we didn't have sex.

I wake the next day with a smile that won't fade, and my excellent mood holds steady throughout the errands I run around town. When I go to the grocery store to pick up some slightly unhealthy staples I plan on hiding from Mom and keeping all to myself, I don't even notice Nate's mother, Tabitha, until she's standing right behind me.

"Long time no see, Sam," she says in that sharp, tinny voice of hers. "I heard you're coming to Nate's wedding."

"Well, it's actually a funny story," I begin, but Tabitha cuts me off.

"It'll be good for you to be there and meet Fiona. She's such a sweetheart," she gushes, putting a hand over her heart. "She's going to make a wonderful wife."

"That's lovely," I tell her, trying to get a word in. "But I'm–"

"It's because she has her priorities straight, you know?" she adds pointedly. "She knows that work is just work, and at the end of the day, her family must come first. Your husband must come first, otherwise, you have no business getting married."

I blink at her, trying to figure out how to respond. I don't want her to lure me into a fight because she doesn't deserve my attention at all, frankly. Also, what's she getting out of bringing this up now? Our marriage ended. I'm out of the picture. You'd think she'd count that as a personal victory. "I thought the point of marriage was to grow old with the person you love," I eventually say. I might not believe in fairy tales, but I know what marriage is supposed to be, and it's not what Nate and I had.

"Hmm, spoken like an expert in marriage," she says with a loud, halting laugh that sounds like an old vacuum cleaner. "How funny."

I glance at the floral department where our chatty neighbor, Mrs. Davis, is picking out a bouquet. Normally, I'd try to avoid her, but right now I'd endure an hour-long conversation about the resale value of her daughter's old Beanie Babies if it would get me out of this awful situation. I try to catch her eye, give her a signal of some kind to come over and save me, but she's still comparing bouquets of lilies and doesn't notice my presence.

"You're not thinking of walking down the aisle again, I hope?" Tabitha asks. "I heard you weren't bringing a date to Nate's wedding, so I just assumed you were single. Still."

As if being single somehow makes me less of a person. What a sour-faced shrew she is. I'm so annoyed by the shade she's hurling at me that I don't even realize what I've said until the words are out. "Actually, I'm bringing my boyfriend, Mylo, to the wedding. I keep forgetting to tell Nate that I'll be using Marty's plus one since Holly can't come." I reach out and squeeze her shoulder in the most patronizing way possible. "Thank you so much for the reminder."

Her dry, mauve-colored lips are still parted wide as I turn away.

"Have a great day, Tabitha," I say with a bright smile, and because I'm on a roll now, "and cute maxi skirt, by the way. You can barely tell how cheap the fabric is." Bitch should've thought twice before coming for me.

Then I head straight for the checkout line as the scene plays over in my mind. Did I really promise to bring Mylo, aka *my boyfriend*, as my date to Nate's wedding? What the fuck have I just done?

CHAPTER 7

MYLO

"*I* feel foolish," I say to Charlie, adjusting the vest that is far too tight around my rib cage. "Do I look foolish?"

"No, my lord," Charlie says in a fake British accent while offering me her best curtsy. "You look exquisite."

We both dressed for the *Bridgerton* theme of our inaugural trivia night. Charlie said others might, and they'll feel better if they see that we are too. Other than the costume being a size too small, I find that I enjoy the fashions of centuries ago. There are far too many layers, but other than that, every piece has impressive detail and accents.

The tailcoat and knee-length trousers are a matching black shade, paired with a black and gold baroque vest, and a loose white shirt has ruffles at the neck that I seem to keep fiddling with. Charlie let me borrow her late grandfather's gold pocket watch as an added accessory.

The event's start time was seven, and by ten after, the lobby is filled with people chatting excitedly about the show, the books, and the differences between the two. A third of the guests are dressed up in Regency attire, which is a pleasant surprise considering how worried I was that Charlie and I would be the only ones sweating. Even Vanessa is wearing a pale yellow, floor-length dress that swishes when she walks.

"Mylo, congrats," she cheers upon arrival. "Look at this turnout. Trivia night is such a good idea."

Axil, trailing behind her, wears a green T-shirt, jeans, and brown work boots.

"You did not dress up," I note with a hint of disappointment.

His tone and expression match mine as he replies, "And you did. I hope you are able to live with that choice."

"It's one night. I think I look dapper," I tell him, confidently tugging on the lapels of my jacket.

"It may be one night," he says, leaning in to whisper, "but the pictures shall last forever."

When he steps away, I see a group of costumed women to my right taking a group photo with the camera aimed in my direction. I am clearly in their shot, but I don't care. This is the theme of the evening, and I want this event to lead to many more, so I shall don this costume proudly.

Zev and Kyan said they would not be able to come, so their absence is expected.

Charlie has trouble sitting down to collect the entry fees given how bulky her gown is, so she remains standing until the crowd starts to thin. I am beside her, handing out small whiteboards and markers to each participating trivia group when Samantha arrives.

She is not dressed for the theme, which I was not expecting anyway, but she looks equally ravishing in her sleeveless, black-and-white striped dress that fits her body like a glove and lands just above her thickly soled black combat boots. The top of her hair is pulled back, leaving a loose strand on either side of her face, and the rest of her tight curls fall around her rounded shoulders.

She shakes her head at the sight of my attire, but the smile that plays on her lips tells me she is impressed by my commitment. "Well done, sir," Samantha says, softly clapping as she reaches me. "You look like you're straight outta Mayfair."

My eyes widen. "You…"

"Yeah, Mom and I started watching the show," she admits sheepishly. "It's better than I thought it would be. It's actually really funny and sharp."

"That's what my dad said when I finally got him to watch," Charlie adds. "He was skeptical at first too." She steps around the table somewhat awkwardly in her long lace-and-flower-covered gown and extends her hand. "Hi, I'm Charlie. I've seen you in here a ton, but we haven't officially met yet."

Samantha shakes it and returns Charlie's smile, which pleases me. I didn't understand the discomfort I sensed from Samantha whenever Charlie's name came up.

"Are you a romance enthusiast yet?" I ask Samantha, knowing that with each book I read to her, the more her resistance wanes.

"Eh," she says with a half-shrug. "I wouldn't use the word enthusiast, but I'm coming around."

I cannot help but beam with pride. "I knew it." Then I decide to test Samantha's emotional investment in *Bridgerton*. "On three, state the name of your favorite character," I say, hoping mine matches hers. "One...two...three—"

At the same time, we both shout, "Lady Danbury."

We chuckle over our shared love of the 'Ton's most clever and impressive resident for a few moments before Samantha looks around the room nervously and clears her throat. How odd.

"How can I help?" she asks. "Since I'm not participating tonight, is there anything I can do?" Opening the black bag at her hip, she pulls out her camera. "I can take photos."

"Wonderful idea," I tell her. Though I don't want her to feel as if she needs to work at this event. I wanted her to come and enjoy herself. "Are you certain you don't mind?"

"Not at all," she says, her face lighting up like a sky full of stars.

Despite the stress of her life as a caregiver, I sense being able to use her photography skills in some way steadies her soul. Bridgerton Trivia Night at the Sudbury Public Library is nothing like the scenes she is used to capturing, I'm sure, but hopefully the event is entertaining to her.

We end up with forty-seven attendees, which far exceeded my

wildest expectations for the night. The group called "Benedict's Broads" comprised of four women in their sixties ends up winning the grand prize—a $20 gift card to Supreme Buns for each of them—but are far more thrilled by their perfect trivia score.

Charlie and I take several pictures with them and their prizes, and the event continues with more lemonade—plus a splash of vodka for those who prefer it—the instrumental songs from the show's sound-track, and light chatter.

Several more selfie requests follow from people who saw the photo Samantha took of me, and though I find the fascination strange, I oblige. Samantha offers to take portraits of everyone in costume and has people stand beneath the arched brick entryway from the lobby to the non-fiction section.

I make my way to the front desk when someone asks to be signed up for a library card, and it is only then that I notice the presence of Officer Burton hovering near the entrance. Encountering him in public is enough to make the hairs rise on the back of my neck but seeing him at my place of work is much more sinister. Why is he here?

"Mr. Monroe," Officer Burton says as he reaches the front desk, spittle already gathering at the corner of his mouth. "Quite the event you've put together here."

Out of the corner of my eye, I notice Charlie weaving her way through the crowd, away from the man in front of me, and while I don't know the reason why she feels compelled to avoid him, I don't blame her. I wish I could be anywhere else at the moment.

"Thank you, Officer Burton," I reply stiffly. This is the man who tried to send my brother to jail for the rest of his life. Granted, it was for a crime Axil did commit, but still. Trevor Burton deserved what he got, and on Sufoi, rape is punishable by death. Though she has not told me herself, I know that not only did Officer Burton's late nephew rape Vanessa but also Samantha.

After Vanessa attempted to report the crime, and Officer Burton manipulated her into thinking it was her fault, Samantha was too afraid to say a word to anyone, knowing no justice would follow.

That is enough to enrage my draxilio, who sends *"Rip out his tongue and nail it to the wall"* in a menacing whisper.

"Mmm," Burton grunts. He scans the room, looking for, I'm not sure what, until his gaze lands on the bottle of vodka in the hands of the frazzled server from Supreme Buns. "Did you apply for a temporary permit to serve that alcohol?" he asks, looking strangely delighted to catch me in what he thinks is a trap.

"I did not," I tell him, straightening my spine. "As there is no charge for it, I didn't think a permit was required." There's no way they can penalize me for a law that simply does not exist.

I detect a hint of disappointment on his face, but then, just as quickly, he turns back to me with his signature sour grin filled with brownish-yellow teeth.

Axil catches my eye from the far corner, and I notice him take Vanessa's hand and pull her behind him toward the doors. They've dealt with enough harassment from this vile, egg-shaped man. I'm glad to see them slip past him.

Officer Burton continues staring at me, saying nothing, just pressing his tongue against the back of his teeth to make a squeaky, slurping sound that is most unpleasant. "Watch yourself now," he eventually says, the warning clear as glass.

Though Luka's hypnosis worked on him well enough to drop the charges against Axil, Officer Burton remains suspicious of me and my brothers, and would love nothing more than to see one or all of us behind bars. We must be extremely careful in his presence.

"Was that Officer Dickmop?" Samantha asks, her small hand wrapping around my bicep.

I cannot help but flex beneath her touch. "Yes, it seems he was trying to find a reason to put an abrupt end to this event."

"Sneaky fucker," she hisses.

"Axil saw him and left with Vanessa right away."

She lets out a pleased sigh. "That's good." Then turns to face me. "Hey, can I speak to you privately for a sec?"

I nod and lead her toward the storage closet on the main floor where we keep the damaged books. It's a meager-sized closet, the shelves packed with books that have missing pages, dented spines, and water damage from the leak in the roof that destroyed dozens of books a few years ago. A mere inch stands between Samantha and me once the door is closed. "What is it?" I worry she is on the verge of ending our arrangement, our "sex friendship" as she calls it. But my worry fades the moment she opens her mouth.

"I need you to come to a wedding with me and pretend to be my boyfriend," she says hurriedly in a single breath.

Inside, I am beaming. Outside, I remain as still as a rock. I want her to say more because she needs something from me and that something is more of my company. It is a delightful feeling to be needed by her.

"Look, I know this is a huge ask," she continues, nervously fidgeting with the silver cuff bracelet on her wrist. "It's just...it's my ex-husband's wedding, and I haven't seen him in a while, and his family is terrible. His mother, in particular, is a huge cu–"

I stop listening to her chaotic babble. She is uncomfortable and there is a hint of fear in her scent and there's nothing I want more than to make it go away. Wrapping my hand around the nape of her neck, I bend down and cover her lips with mine. Samantha moans as she sags against me, her perfect, ample flesh beneath my hands. She is right where she belongs.

Yesss, my draxilio cheers. *Mate. Our mate.*

Startled that my thoughts would even remotely align with his desires, I jerk back. Samantha's magnificent mouth is swollen from my kiss, and her brown eyes swirl with heat as they slowly blink open.

"Um," I begin, trying to settle myself, "I would be delighted to be your pretend boyfriend." Then I gesture to the door. "We should get back out there before someone notices we're gone."

She follows me out, saying "Uh, thank you" from behind me.

Charlie meets us at the front desk and tells us the last of the guests have left. Samantha helps the frazzled sub shop server with her catering cleanup while Charlie and I collect the empty cups and white-boards and return the folded chairs to the book closet.

Samantha gets a text from Vanessa telling us to meet her, Axil, and Zev at Tipsy's Bar. I invite Charlie to join us, but she declines, saying she needs to get home. Samantha and I lock up, setting the alarm as we go, and find ourselves alone in a dark, quiet parking lot. She looks me up and down and says, "Is that what you're wearing to the bar?"

I had not considered going anywhere but home after trivia ended. "I don't have other clothes, so yes."

She glances at a swath of pine trees that blocks the Sudbury Animal Hospital from view. "Could we...fly to Tipsy's?" she asks shyly.

It is not an unreasonable question, I suppose. During the chilly days of winter, I have commuted to work via my draxilio on more than one occasion. But I have certainly never flown with anyone, and I'm not sure I should start now. It is one thing for Sam to know of our true forms, and for me to unmask in front of her when we have sex. It is quite another to shift into my draxilio in her presence and offer her a ride in my claws.

Being in this form, my flightless form, I am in control. The way I behave around Samantha is measured, controlled, and with the ever-present goal of a male who seeks to pleasure and be pleasured in return. If I allow my draxilio to take charge, especially in the vicinity of Samantha, I'm not sure what he'll do. He sees her as his mate. What if he decides this is his only chance to claim her and he flies off, taking her several states away?

"Please?" she begs. She actually begs with her palms pressed together and her eyes wide, vulnerable, and needy. The seam of her hands is nestled between her breasts, and I notice the cool night air has caused her nipples to harden beneath her dress. My tongue runs along the edge of my teeth as I envision taking her nipple between my lips and sucking on it until she writhes beneath me.

"Of course," I reply instantly, unable to shake the image and the power it has over me. I just hope my draxilio minds his manners on this flight.

CHAPTER 8

MYLO

"Just...do me a kindness, yes?" I say as I lead her into a small clearing between the trees. It is dense enough here to hide even the massive, winged beast I become when I shift, and once my feet leave the ground, the invisibility cloak every draxilio has activates and will protect us from anyone who happens to be gazing at the stars tonight. Getting caught in my other form is not what worries me.

"Sure," Samantha says, eager to return the favor I have just granted.

"If my draxilio does anything," I begin, struggling to find the right way to phrase this, "if he behaves in a way that makes you feel uncomfortable or unsafe, I want you to hit him as hard as you can."

She blinks several times before laughter bursts from her. This continues for far longer than I think appropriate for a warning so serious before she notices I'm not laughing with her. "You're kidding, right?"

"No, I am not kidding."

Samantha steps toward me, her smile warm as she places her hands on my chest. "Mylo, there's no way your dragon would hurt me."

How can she be so sure? During my time on Sufoi, I was a highly skilled assassin for the king. The dark, grisly acts I have committed, and still capable of, would surely give Samantha nightmares. "You have not seen this other side of me, Samantha, and it would be unwise to underestimate a creature the size of a tall building who can breathe fire."

But my sex friend is not the least bit swayed by my words.

"Nope. I don't buy it." She shakes her head and glides one hand to the middle of my chest. My draxilio begins to purr, and her smile widens when she feels the vibration of it through my clothes. "See? He likes me. I trust him."

I go to argue with her, but she grabs my chin and pulls it down until my eyes meet hers.

"More importantly, I trust *you*," she adds.

I panic briefly at the thought of my eyes turning blood red indicating that Samantha is my true mate, and I wonder how she would respond. Compared to Luka's and Axil's mates' reactions, this would surely end in a better result since Samantha already knows I am part draxilio. However, she has said that she has no interest in entering another long-term committed relationship. How quickly would she run upon learning she's my true mate?

Thankfully, the intense itching that comes with the red eyes never occurs. Just to be safe, though, I take off my glasses. "D-do my eyes look normal?" I ask her, my voice shaky at the possibility that they're currently the color of crimson.

"Yup," she says without hesitation. "As gray as ever."

Breath whooshes out of me as I silently thank my draxilio for not complicating my existence further. "Very well." With renewed energy, I gesture for Samantha to step back and give me plenty of room. I close my eyes and envision my draxilio with his shimmering scales, his dagger-sharp teeth, and his wide, thick wings as they cut through passing clouds. I feel the pull of my skin as the shift takes hold, and the cracking of bones when his much stronger ones replace mine. Within a heartbeat or two, I am transformed.

"Wow," Samantha says with a gasp. Her hands cover her heart as she tentatively steps closer.

Friend, I remind my draxilio from deep within his mind. *She is your friend. Not your mate. Do not scare her.*

I would plummet to my death before causing her even a moment of fear, he sends back, annoyed.

But I don't care. He needs to hear this. *Care for her. Be gentle. Do not push.*

I do not need to, he sends back, confidence thick in his tone. *She will choose us.*

I don't agree with him, nor do I want to agree with him since Samantha and I are not mates.

Sex friends, I remind him. *That is all.*

He ignores me as he uncurls his claw and she steps inside, taking a seat in the center. He holds her tight enough so she is secure, but not too tight that she struggles to move. Then he launches into the night sky, and I hear her shouting with glee as she takes in the sight of her hometown far below.

The flight to Tipsy's lasts about two minutes as Sudbury is a very small place, and there is no resistance from my draxilio when I shift back.

Good job, I send to him. *I am proud of you.*

Leave me be, he sends back with a growl. *Focus your attention on her.*

We stroll casually out of the woods near Tipsy's and make our way toward the entrance.

"Told you," she mutters over her shoulder. "He likes me."

"That was never in question," I remind her, swinging open the door.

The bass thumps loudly through the speakers as we enter, and a low, melodic voice sings a familiar tune. I recognize it as a song that I'm certain Zev has played for me, but I cannot place the song's name or even the singer.

"Oh my god," Samantha beams as we maneuver through the crowd. "Yes, love Adele."

Adele, that is it. Zev cannot get enough of her.

And the version being sung now, while not as impressive as Adele's, is surprisingly close.

"There you are," Vanessa shouts from her seat at the bar. She waves us over and pulls Samantha into a tight hug.

Zev pats me on the back and hands me a glass of beer. I cannot tell what kind, but I'm certain I will not like it. "You may keep that," I tell him before leaning over the bar and catching Izzy's attention. "May I have a mint mojito? The drink you made for me last time I was here."

Izzy smiles. "I knew you were a mojito guy. Comin' right up."

As the owner of the bar, you would think Izzy would have trouble remembering all the customers' names and which drinks they prefer, but not Izzy. The barkeep's memory is as sharp as my draxilio's teeth. A man and woman I have not seen before are behind the bar, working alongside Izzy to pour drinks, which is good. A crowd this size would be tricky to serve with just one person.

"Isn't she amazing?" Vanessa says loudly over the noise of the crowd. She points to the singer standing on a wide black platform, which serves as a makeshift stage.

Her statuesque radiance is striking, along with her intricately woven blonde hairstyle that is piled atop her head, the bright red color of her sequined dress that matches her lips, and the gold, black, and white shades around her eyes. "Who is she?"

"Oh, that's Uma Sinner," Izzy says with a proud chuckle. "By day, he's my accountant, Paul Rossi, and by night, he transforms into Uma Sinner, the most popular drag queen in Tilton. I asked her to come perform tonight, and miraculously, she was available."

"Wait," I say. "He or she? I am confused."

Izzy points at Uma. "*She* when she's Uma. *He* when he's Paul. Make sense?"

I nod. "Yes, thank you for explaining."

Izzy gives me an appreciative nod while filling a bowl with peanuts and pushing it toward us.

"Zev, what is this song?" I lean in to ask him. "I have heard it before, yes?"

"Yeah, it's *Rolling in the Deep* by Adele," he says. "I've played it on the piano."

Ah, that is how I know it, because of how many times he practiced it.

"Oh shit! Come on, Vanilla," Samantha suddenly cheers.

She and Vanessa are hand-in-hand when they leave the bar and scurry into the center of the floor to dance. The song has changed, and again, I do not recognize it. I should listen to more music, clearly. "What is this one called?" I ask Zev.

"This is *Flowers* by Miley Cyrus."

Though I have not heard the original version, Uma sings it beautifully.

When Samantha starts to dance, I cannot make my eyes look elsewhere. She is far too dazzling. Her hips sway in a steady rhythm that leaves me hypnotized. The way her breasts bounce and her stomach jiggles as she moves leaves my mouth dry enough that I throw back my mojito in two large sips. "Another, please," I say to Izzy, who nods and takes my empty glass and pours a fresh one.

The only time my attention drifts from Samantha's spectacular body is when a man I do not recognize inches closer to her. My fists clench at my sides when she notices him and starts shaking her ass against his cock. A cock that thankfully is concealed by dark denim, but still, it is far too close to her for my comfort.

Destroy him, my draxilio urges.

But I cannot. As tempted as I am to reach down this man's throat and pull out his spine, I must refrain. Samantha is my sex friend. Nothing more.

"Are you well, Mylo?" Zev asks, his eyes boring into mine as he waits for my next move.

Unclenching my teeth, I reply, "Fine."

Axil growls steadily to my right as the man behind Samantha moves to dance with both her and Vanessa. My brother pushes himself off the bar and marches straight over, then stands perfectly still, glowering at the man until he saunters away.

Vanessa leans into her mate, giving him a playful smack on the arm, and when the song ends, they all return to the bar. Samantha stands next to me, and the possessive need I felt pumping through my blood a moment ago has me reaching out, just a finger, to the small hand that hangs an inch away. The distance between us is too much, and I shift my weight onto my right foot, closing the space that separates our bodies just enough for my pinky to lightly brush against the back of her hand.

Her hand turns over, and her pinky entwines with mine. Still, it is not enough. My need for her is like wildfire tearing through my bones, and the only relief is her touch.

"Mylo," Vanessa calls, holding up my mojito, "your drink."

Samantha rips her hand from my grasp and pretends to yawn, stretching her arms over her head in such an obvious way that seems like it would elicit more questions than holding my hand in the first place would have, but we are in public, I must remember, and the moment has passed.

Izzy calls me over to a spot at the end of the bar and I step away from Samantha to chat. "You know, Uma has a break in her schedule next month." The Tipsy owner dries a glass and sets it on the bar. "You should see if she's free to do a story time session at the library for the kids. Vanessa said your trivia night was a success, and you're looking to have more events."

I turn to face the stage and notice Uma has stepped down to the floor, mingling with the crowd as she sings. Her energy is palpable, and no one in the audience can take their eyes off her. Likewise, there is not a frown to be found in all of Tipsy's. Uma's warmth radiates like a halo as she engages with each person she passes. She is accessible and jovial while also maintaining queen-like poise. I cannot imagine a better person to hold the attention of a group of squirming children.

"Apologies that I do not know much about drag queens," I confess to Izzy. "Would she even be interested in doing such a thing?"

"Oh yeah," Izzy says. "Drag story hour is a thing. She's done it before."

How kind of Izzy to seek me out and offer ways to improve the library with no reason to do so, apart from wanting to help me.

I had hoped this was something I would get from Councilman Grady, the new city councilman who oversees this ward and has repeatedly denied my budget requests. Or, if not ideas on how to improve the facility, then an interest in the ideas I provide.

But no, it is clear he sees the library as a mere drain on government resources, even when he refuses to use funds to repair parts of the building that are falling apart. I invited him to trivia night, but unsurprisingly, he did not show his face. I'm not sure he even lives in the ward he is charged with managing.

"Thank you, Izzy. I shall see if Uma is interested."

Uma eventually takes a break from singing to have a drink at the bar, and I take that as an opportunity to discuss story hour with her.

"Hel-lo there," she says, her eyes drifting over my attire. She glances at Izzy, filling her glass with ice cubes and dark liquor. "Is this the Viscount of Sudbury?"

Izzy laughs. "That's actually our head librarian. Uma, meet Mylo. Mylo, Uma."

Uma extends her hand in a way that indicates I should kiss it, and I do, with a bow. "Pleasure to meet you, Miss Uma Sinner."

She laughs heartily at my excessive chivalry and pats the stool next to her. "Take a seat, gorgeous. What can I do for you?"

I explain my idea, Izzy's idea, rather, and tell her about the group of ten or so children that frequent my weekly story time. "They are wonderful kids, and I want to make sure they remain excited about reading. It seems far too easy for students to fall out of love with books the older they get and the more material they are forced to read."

"Oof, so true. I still detest *Romeo and Juliet* because of how many essays I had to write about it in school," she tells me before throwing back her drink in one large sip. "I mean, killing yourself over one man. It doesn't get any dumber than that. And Juliet was a total smoke show. She could've had at least three new boyfriends if she waited a day."

"Precisely," I say with a laugh. "Would you consider coming to read to the kids? I know your time is in great demand, but anytime you are free, the Sudbury Library is available to you."

"Sure thing, honey," she says. "I'll give you a discount, too, since you're a friend of Izzy's."

Even if I were to use the measly sum provided annually by city council for special events, it would not cover Uma's discounted rate. But this is important, and I know the kids will love it.

"Fund the library yourself," Kyan suggested.

As much as I hate when he is right, I'm about to do just that.

"Splendid," I tell Uma.

We are in the middle of discussing potential dates and times when the music stops, and a hush falls over the crowd.

"Fucking hell," I hear Izzy grumble, stomping toward the other end of the bar near the entrance.

Standing there, I see Officer Burton with four other officers gathered behind him. Izzy approaches them and has what looks to be a heated exchange with Officer Burton. Eventually, Izzy's expression goes from murderous to resigned, taking a slip of paper from Officer Burton. The officers leave immediately after that.

Izzy takes the stage, paper in hand, and grabs the mic. "Okay, guys. So, we've received a noise complaint." The crowd boos and hisses. Izzy's eyes roll in agreement. "Yeah, I know. Considering the closest building houses a dentist's office that is currently closed, I think we all know what this is about."

"Mmm-hmm," Uma groans. "Different circus, same clownery."

The crowd offers their own exasperated agreement. None of which I understand.

"For the rest of the night, we'll switch back to one of our beloved playlists here at Tipsy's, but let's give the almighty Uma Sinner a round of applause for her amazing performance tonight."

Uma stands and bows several times as the crowd continues clapping. Cheers and whistles also accompany the applause. Uma and I exchange numbers before she leaves and despite the return of the music, the mood inside the bar has soured.

People begin to leave, and our group follows suit. Samantha gives Izzy a hug, and I have Axil explain to me what he has seen in the news recently about prejudice against drag queens as we walk outside. The conversation leaves me with more questions than answers, but that is to be expected, considering how prejudice is rarely rooted in logic.

"I shall walk you home," I whisper to Samantha when the rest of the group is ahead of us.

"No," she replies quickly. "That's okay. My house is closer than yours. I'll be fine."

"Are you guys coming?" Vanessa hollers from several feet in front of us.

I do not like the idea of Samantha walking home unaccompanied, but if she refuses my escort, there's not much else I can do.

"We'll be right there," Samantha shouts back, then she tugs me over near the dumpster behind Tipsy's.

"Look," she starts, avoiding my gaze. "What happened earlier can't happen again."

What does she speak of? The kiss in the book closet? Her request to act as her fake boyfriend?

"The hand holding," she finally says.

Ah, that. "So I am to act as your boyfriend, but only in front of certain people. Is that right?"

"Well, yeah. I don't want Vanessa and your brothers knowing about this because they'll never let it go until we're married," she says, the word like acid on her tongue. "Is that what you want, Mylo? Marriage? Living your life for someone else?"

Yes, my draxilio purrs.

I pause. Even inside my own head, there is not a clear answer. Not long ago, my response would have been a resounding no, or at the very least, not yet, but now, when I think of marriage, my mind grows murky.

As I was never able to picture someone specific to share my life with, the idea of it seemed too vague, too laborious a task to pique my interest. But when Samantha says the word "marriage," hers is the face I see at my side. It is the comfort and warmth of her hand I would seek out on my most trying days. It is her body I would worship until my final breath. And none of that would feel like work. It would be...easy.

"Of course not," I lie, because it's clearly what she wants to hear.

"Me either," she replies firmly. "What we have now is great, just the way it is. In order to keep it that way, this," she gestures between us, "needs to remain a secret."

"Right."

"But in two weeks, at my ex's wedding..." her voice takes on a throaty, coy tone, "you're my boyfriend. My hands will be wherever you want them to be."

She grabs my chin and pulls me down to her level, then offers me a quick brush of her lips before she saunters away and into the night. While my blood burns to run after her and hold her against a tree as I thrust into her hot cunt, I steady my breaths and tell myself that I will not have to wait long. In front of our friends, we must act like we are nothing, but in private, and at this upcoming wedding, her body is mine to ravish.

CHAPTER 9

SAM

"I don't know about this one," I say to Vanessa as I adjust the tulle skirt of my dress. It's the fourth one I've tried on, and so far, none seem right for Nate's wedding, which is now less than a week away. I'm incredibly distracted and irritable due to my lack of sleep this past week. Mom has started sleepwalking, and I've gotten a total of eight hours of solid shut-eye in the last six days. Dress shopping is the last thing I want to be doing, especially since none of these dresses look good on me. "It's too froofy, I think."

Vanessa tilts her head from side to side as her brow furrows. "Yeah, it's not you. Your style is more edgy and bold, and this is…" she gestures at the embroidered roses covering the bottom half of the dress made from glittery beads.

"More *Bridgerton*-y?" I offer.

"Yes," Vanessa exclaims. "Wait, are you finally reading the books?" Before I answer, she shakes her head with a pleased smirk. "I've been trying to get you to read them for years."

"No, not reading the books," I clarify. "But Mom and I are watching the show."

"Isn't it so good?" she asks.

I nod.

She eyes me closely for a moment, then her jaw falls open. "Wait, is this because of Mylo's trivia night? Did you start watching it because of him?"

Shit, shit, shit. I shouldn't have even mentioned *Bridgerton*. What was I thinking? Although, I did see her and Axil at trivia night. Would it really be unheard of for me to see how much fun everyone had and start watching it on my own? It's not as if admitting I started watching because of Mylo is the same as admitting we're sleeping together.

Still, though, I don't want to drop any breadcrumbs to our secret fling that Vanessa would feel compelled to follow.

"Did I start watching one of the most popular shows on Netflix because of a boy?" I ask, my tone dripping with sarcasm. "No, girl. I'm watching it for the sex scenes just like everyone else."

She shrugs. "Fair enough." Then points to the dress hanging behind the rest I picked to try on. "I have a good feeling about the purple halter dress. Put that one on next."

I do as she asks, grateful the subject of *Bridgerton* has been dropped. Heading back into the dressing room, I pull off the ball gown and tug the halter dress over my head. The color is a dusty, dark purple, and the top is a cross-halter style that meets at the base of my throat, leaving my back and shoulders bare, and the silk fabric wraps delicately around my boobs, making them look bigger than they are, which I love. The skirt is more textured but hugs my hips and ass in a flattering silhouette, with a cut-out placed just above my ribs and a slit that reaches mid-thigh, giving it a more modern flair. Plus, this shade of purple really pops with my skin tone and dark brown hair.

"Yup, this is the one," I tell Vanessa as I step out of the dressing room and give her a spin.

"Oh hell yeah," she says with an awestruck clap. "You look hot, Samwich."

I flip my hair over my shoulder and pose like Beyoncé. "Why thank you, Vanilla."

Vanessa waits as I pay for the dress, and we continue strolling through the clothing store as we chat about the wedding. "I can't figure it out," Vanessa says. "Like, why would he want his ex-wife to meet his new wife? It's not like you guys have kids or any other reason to remain in each other's lives."

"I guess I'll have to solve the mystery once I'm there."

"And you're going with Marty?" she asks. "It's good you won't be alone, at least."

"Right."

Vanessa is the best friend I've got, and I hate lying to her, but this is a necessary evil if I want to keep seeing Mylo. And I do. Mom has had more bad days than good lately, and our secret meetups are the only thing keeping me sane.

"Ugh, this baby is sucking more energy out of my body every day. Can we sit?" she asks when we make it to the shoe department. She plops down on a green velvet bench meant for people trying on shoes and lets out a deep exhale. "You know what's worse? He or she has obliterated my sex drive. It's nothing like it used to be, and I'm praying it'll go back to normal in the next trimester."

I sit next to her. "I'm sure it will." I have no idea if it will or not, but Vanessa clearly needs positive reinforcement right now.

"What I don't understand," she leans in closer and whispers, "is why I suddenly need lube during sex. Before pregnancy, I was like a damn fire hose. Now? Extreme drought." She shakes her head. "It doesn't make sense. You'd think with all the fluids passing back and forth between me and the baby, there'd be plenty extra to…" she speaks out of the corner of her mouth, "saturate the garden, if you know what I mean."

Of course, I know what she means. Anyone over age ten would know what she means. "I don't think pregnancy works like that," I say with an amused chuckle, "but I'm sorry about your dry vag situation. That blows."

"It really does. Though, I am glad to be rid of my period for a while."

That's the only part of her pregnancy I'm jealous of. "Agreed," I tell her. "I'm sick of my period. At thirty-seven, I feel like I shouldn't have to go through this much bloating and pain on a monthly basis. It's been over twenty years. Enough already."

"I know, right?" Vanessa mutters with a smirk as she picks up a platform furry Ugg slipper. She looks through the boxes beneath the display slipper, trying to find her size. She pulls one box from the bottom of the pile and kicks off her Allbirds sneakers to try them on. "You can always get pregnant if you'd like an extended break from it."

"Pass," I say with a scoff. "Motherhood is not for me." I scan through the shoes on display in this area of the store, looking for a pair that would go well with the dress I just bought, but also won't kill my feet which is a tall order for a dressy shoe. "I've thought about getting my tubes tied, or a hysterectomy—whichever one makes it so I wouldn't get my period anymore, and I'd never have to worry about an accidental pregnancy."

"Makes sense," Vanessa says, kicking up her feet in the slippers and wiggling her toes. "If you don't want kids, why put your fate in the hands of birth control pills and condoms, right?"

"Exactly."

Her gaze meets mine, and it's filled with warmth. "If you make that appointment, I'll go with you, if you want."

"Thank you," I tell her. The rest of what I want to say is implied. *Thank you for not asking if I'm sure that I don't want kids. Thank you for not cautioning me that I might want them in the future, or if I met the right guy.* And *thank you for offering to hold my hand while I endure a procedure that is sure to be just as inconvenient and uncomfortable as my period is every month.* I don't know what I'd do without her.

"What about your little one?" I ask, eager to shift the conversation away from the emotions bubbling up inside me. "When's your next sonogram?"

"Luka, Harper, and Ryan are coming up in a couple of weeks to stay with us. They'll do it then."

"Will you learn the sex?"

"Maybe," Vanessa says. "It might be too early, but both of Harper's pregnancies were about seven months, so dragon babies apparently cook a little faster."

My phone vibrates inside my purse, and Marty's name flashes across the screen as I answer it. "Yo. Mom okay?"

"Yeah, she's taking a nap. I'm looking for the Reese's Cup bunnies I left in the cabinet above the fridge. They're not here."

"Because I ate them."

"Okay," he mutters, irritated. "And the mini-Snickers bars I hid in the pantry?"

"Yup, ate those too."

"What about the fruit roll-ups I put in the back of the bread box? Or the snickerdoodle cookies I stuffed inside that roasted seaweed bag?"

"Yeah, those are both gone."

"What the fuck, Sam? I left that stuff here so that I'd have something to snack on during my Sunday shifts."

Perhaps I should feel a little bad, but I don't. Perhaps I'm still punishing Marty for making me go to Nate's wedding. I don't feel bad about that either. "My house, my snacks."

"Seriously? You had to eat all sixteen cookies? You couldn't leave me one?"

"Look, man, we're trying to make sure Mom eats clean, are we not? I'm just doing my part to eliminate temptation for her."

He grunts angrily into the phone. "Fine. You mess with my stuff; I'm messing with yours." I hear the creak of the floorboards as he marches up the steps and down the hall toward my room. Then a stream of quiet expletives falls out of his mouth when he's unable to open the door.

"Ha, nice try, bitch," I say, tauntingly. "You think I'm dumb enough to leave my room unlocked when you're there?"

"This isn't over," he warns. I hear him try turning the handle again, the hinges on the door squeaking as he tries slamming his shoulder into it, and eventually, he sighs in defeat. "Can you at least bring me home some candy?"

I concede, but only a little. "If Vanessa and I happen to stop at a store that sells candy, I will get you some."

"You can't just make an extra stop to get me something?"

He is such a giant baby. "Who am I, your wife? No," I tell him with a laugh. "Take your snacks home with you at the end of the day if you don't want me eating them."

Marty swears under his breath as he hangs up.

Vanessa looks entertained despite having only heard my side of the conversation.

I shrug. "Brothers."

"Hey, wanna come back to my place and help set up the nursery?" Vanessa asks. "Axil just finished building the crib, and we've had some other furniture delivered."

"Sure," I tell her. "Mind dropping me off at my place after?"

"Not at all."

When we arrive at Vanessa's, Zev and Kyan are putting together a tall white dresser and squabbling over the instructions while Mylo and Axil are unwrapping the crib mattress.

"Wow, is this the crib?" I ask as we enter the room. Axil made the baby bed by hand, and it's as much of a masterpiece as the rest of the furniture he's made. The wood is a rich brown color—I'm not sure what kind of wood it is—but tiny birds and squirrels are carved into the bars in the front, flowers and happy-faced suns run along the bar across the top, and the entire back panel features a cute woodland scene with owls, bears, and a fox peacefully existing alongside one another. "It's gorgeous, Axil."

"Many thanks, Sam," he says in his usual deadpan growl.

My eyes drift to the dresser, which now looks extremely boring and shoddy in comparison. "I'm surprised you didn't make all the nursery furniture by hand."

"If it were up to Axil, he would have," Vanessa says with a loving eye roll.

He grunts. "I was not given enough time before you started ordering things." Axil looks over at the dresser with disgust. "This is temporary. We shall use it until I can put together a better one."

"How was shopping?" Zev asks, seemingly eager for an excuse to stop assembling the cheap furniture.

Vanessa whistles. "You guys should see this dress Sam bought for the wedding she's going to. It's a heart-stopper."

"Is that so?" Mylo asks, his mouth curving into a wicked grin. "I'd love to see this dress."

What the hell is he doing, teasing me in front of everyone? Or, on second thought, Mylo is a natural flirt. Maybe it'd be more suspect if he didn't.

All right then. Two can play this game. "I doubt you could handle it."

He sits up straighter, an arrogant glint in his eye. "Really." More statement than question. "I assure you, Samantha, I'm quite capable of handling anything."

"Even a backless dress..." I say, tucking my chin against my shoulder and turning to the side, my lips forming a perfect pout. "Made of silk as soft as butter. A dress that's impossible to wear a bra with and has a slit that comes up to..." I run a finger from my knee slowly up my thigh, "here?"

Mylo audibly swallows as his heavy-lidded eyes remain on my upper thigh. The tension in the room is thicker than blood, and I worry I've taken this game too far. But then Mylo shakes himself free of my spell and stands. "Your dress could be covered in a million thumbtacks, Samantha," he rasps as he steps closer, "and one moment alone is all I'd need to turn it into a pile of rags on the floor."

Fuck, I curse silently, knowing my panties are probably soaked. He's better at this than I thought. Never underestimate a librarian. I need to remember that.

"Your date to this wedding is quite a lucky fellow," he says, shooting me a wink that only I can see and returning to his seat next to the crib.

"She's actually going with her brother," Vanessa points out.

"What a shame," he says. "You should've asked me."

Okay, this is getting too real. I need to dump a metaphorical bucket of cold water on this whole conversation. And yet...teasing Mylo is just too much fun. I can't seem to help myself. "I don't know. I can't picture you as much of a dancer. Any wedding date of mine will need to dance."

"I'm an excellent dancer," he replies, leaning back in the chair and putting his hands behind his head. "You might struggle to keep up with me, in fact."

Zev and Kyan both let out a comical "Ooh!" as if Mylo has delivered a soul-crushing retort.

That sound, not just a reminder of their presence in the room, but their active participation in the flirtatious exchange between me and Mylo is what brings reality crashing down. If they were suspicious of us before, they must be certain of it now. How could they not? Mylo and I have teased each other in the past, but never like this. Never with such heat, and never blurring the line between truth and fiction like we just did.

I need to get out of here before I let something slip. "I guess we'll never know," I mumble as I grab my purse and dress off the floor of the nursery. Pulling Vanessa in for an awkward hug that she wasn't expecting, I say goodbye to her and the boys before racing out of the room.

"Wait, didn't you want a ride home?" she yells after me.

"Nah, I'll walk!" I shout back. "I need my daily walk."

Exhausted and embarrassed, I cut through the cemetery and make it home before the sun sets. I kick off my white platform Keds by the door and find the living room empty. Then I climb the stairs with a huff, and upon unlocking my bedroom door, I toss my purse on my desk chair, carefully hang my dress in the closet, and connect my phone to the charger on my nightstand.

Marty is just coming out of the bathroom when I step out into the hall, and before I can say anything, he puts a finger to his lips. "Shh, Ma's still asleep." Then he looks down at my empty hands. "Bring me anything?"

"No," I say with a groan as I follow him downstairs and plunk down on the couch. "I don't know why you expected me to after I told you I wasn't going to."

"Eh, you know. Expect the worst, hope for the best." He takes a seat in Mom's chair and flips through the channels aimlessly. "You ready for the wedding?"

I let out a sigh. "I guess." His mention of the wedding reminds me of something. "I'm taking your plus one, by the way. I was going to let Nate know that I was bringing a date, but you RSVP'd with Holly coming, right? And now she's not?"

"Yeah, that's true. I guess you could just take her spot. But…who are you taking?"

"Mylo Monroe," I reply easily. "The guy who runs the library." Since my siblings don't often interact with Vanessa and the guys, and since Marty is about to meet him in a matter of days, there's no point in hiding it from him.

"The story time guy whose shirts are too tight?" he asks with a sneer.

"His shirts aren't too tight." It's not Mylo's fault if the largest size offered at most stores is still too small to accommodate his spectacularly large body.

"Oh, by the way," Marty says, clearing his throat. "What do you think about adding a gate to the top of the stairs?"

"A gate?"

"Yeah, like a baby gate. For Mom. Jackie and I were talking yesterday about putting in a few safeguards around here. As…you know, Mom progresses."

"I mean, I guess we could do that."

I understand the need to make this place a little safer as she often gets confused about where things are, but when I picture her reaction to a baby gate, I see only frustration. "Don't you think a baby gate would just be a glaring reminder of her disease?" I point out.

"Well, today I put a mini-fridge in her room, so she doesn't have to go up and down the stairs whenever she needs a sip of water from the Brita," Marty says. "She seemed happy about that change."

Looking at the position of her favorite chair, she'd be able to see the gate clearly at the top of the steps whenever she's watching TV, which is most of the time. "Yeah, well, that makes sense and makes her life easier. The gate is different. It'll upset her. Do we really want to create more opportunities for her to be upset? I thought we were trying to reduce her stress."

"Hmm," Marty mutters as he considers this. "That's a good point. Though we'll probably have to revisit this." He runs a rough hand through his wavy black hair. "There's gonna come a day when we'll have to put her safety above her happiness. We can't avoid it."

I stare at the edge of the carpet as I let his words sink in. It's really only going to get worse from here on out, isn't it?

"Holly suggested hiring a nurse. You know, someone who could be here with her all the time." He turns to me. "Then you wouldn't have to take on as much."

What could he mean by that? Is he hinting that I haven't been doing a good job? That we need an outsider to be here with Mom because I can't be trusted to take care of her? Maybe Jackie told him how I let her watch *Real Housewives*. Or that I haven't been as strict with her diet as she was. So, I've let her eat some of her favorite meals without cutting out the salt entirely. So what? She should be able to enjoy the food she eats while she still can.

Though, he said Holly made the suggestion. Which, frankly, she has no business doing in the first place. We're her family by marriage, not by blood, and we don't need to drain the rest of my savings to hire a nurse to come in and do what I'm already doing. I'm down to just four-hundred dollars in my savings account right now, and that's all I have until I start working again.

Besides, being able to care for Mom is my responsibility. I'm able to make up for all the time I've lost while I was out on the road. I'm not going to let some stranger take that from me.

"I'm doing fine," I tell him. "The setup we have now is fine. I have the weekends to decompress, and that's all I need. We don't need someone else coming in here to take care of Mom. She has enough trouble remembering who we are."

Marty nods but remains quiet. He flips through the channels once more, and eventually hands me the remote and says he needs to head home. "We can talk more about the baby gate with Jackie. I'll let her know what you said, though."

In other words, Jackie wants to install the baby gate, and that means the baby gate *will* be installed at some point. Whenever Jackie gets an idea in her head, she runs with it until the issue is resolved to her satisfaction. Even if said idea involves Marty or me, what Jackie says goes. It's always been that way. She's three inches shorter than me and can't weigh more than a hundred twenty pounds soaking wet, and she still finds a way to boss us all around. It must be an oldest-child thing.

Mom wakes up a half hour later, yawning as she walks slowly down the hall. I race up the stairs to guide her down, and the moment her eyes land on me, she smiles so brightly that it lights up her entire face. "Rosa, you're here." As soon as her feet touch the carpet on the first floor, she pulls me into a tight hug. So tight I can barely breathe. "I've missed you so much."

Rosa was Mom's younger sister. She died eight years ago after a long battle with lung cancer. I know she was around a lot when I was a baby, but her visits became less frequent once she got a job as a flight attendant. From the many stories I heard growing up, Rosa lived a full, wild life. She never married or had kids but was always visiting one of the many boyfriends she had spread across the globe.

I remember four distinct things about her: she loved owls so much she had one tattooed on her hip, her favorite drink was a whiskey on the rocks, she had a massive crush on John Travolta, and always had a pack of cigarettes in her purse.

Mom told me more than once that I looked like her, and right now, she seems to think I am her.

Part of me wants to tell her the truth, and perhaps that's what I should do. But that would mean revealing her sister is dead, and I can't stomach seeing that heartbroken look on her face right now. The one that steals the color from her cheeks the moment she realizes her disease has, once again, played a trick on her mind.

There's gonna come a day when we'll have to put her safety above her happiness. Marty's words from earlier float back to me. However, playing along with Mom's current version of reality wouldn't put her in any danger. Certainly not physical danger, anyway. And I'm sure not even in a mental or emotional sense, really. I mean, will she even remember this exchange in the morning? Probably not.

If only for today, I want her to live inside the memory that her mind has brought forth. There's happiness there. I see it as clear as day in her smile.

"I missed you too," I tell her, taking on the role of Rosa. "It's good to see you."

"*Dios mío,* look at you," she says, pulling back to hold my face in her hands. "Still have the smooth skin of a newborn baby." Mom sits next to me on the couch and takes my hands in hers. "Tell me, how has life been treating you?"

I have no idea what year she thinks it is, or how long it's been in her mind since she's seen Rosa, so I have to be careful here. Anything out of the ordinary could shatter the memory and force Mom back into the present.

"Uh, good," I tell her, trying to ease the shakiness out of my voice. Rosa was confident as hell, and that's what I need to be. "You know, same old, same old. A new day, a new city, a new man. What could be better than that?"

Mom barks out a laugh and playfully smacks my knee. "Ay, *nena,* you're wild. I love it."

She sits there, quietly smiling at me for a moment before she pats my leg again. "Do you remember that summer when we snuck out during la Noche de San Juan to meet the boys down the street from Abuelita's house to skinny-dip in the ocean?"

My mother sneaking out to go skinny-dipping with boys? Adorable. And a story she definitely never would've shared with me, at least not while I was young enough to do the same.

"I do, yeah," I say with a nostalgic sigh. "That was a crazy night."

"Not as crazy as when we got those tattoos!"

Tattoo? I had no idea my mom had a tattoo. Shit, is she going to ask to see the owl on my hip? I hope not. Maybe if I keep the focus on her, the owl won't come up. "Where did you get yours again? I can't remember."

She wags a finger at me. "All that ayahuasca is melting your brain cells."

Jesus Christ. Aunt Rosa did ayahuasca?

Mom reaches for the hem of her nightgown and lifts it to expose her upper thigh. There, about an inch lower than her panty line is the faded silhouette of a wolf with its snout lifted toward the sky as if howling at the moon.

"Remember now?" she says with a chuckle as she tugs her nightgown back into place.

I wish I did. I wish I was there when she got it, and I wish I knew why she chose a wolf, of all things. What does that symbolize for her, I wonder? As tempted as I am to ask her, I worry I'm already treading water after not remembering what she got in the first place. "I do. It still looks good as new."

We chat like this for, I don't know how long, with me asking Mom about her favorite memories of childhood, and Mom sharing stories I've never heard before. She lets out a loud snort as she laughs through her tale about how she and Rosa snuck into a Menudo concert and flashed Ricky Martin. I learn about Mom's brief stint as a card dealer at a casino, and she speaks fondly of her grandmother, who seemed incredibly strict, but was also a gifted cook.

"How long are you home for?" Mom asks, leaning in and taking my hands once more. "A while?"

Her dark brown eyes swirl with hope, and her smile is so light, so free of any burden, that I wish I could grab my phone and take a picture of her without her noticing. I want to remember her just like this. Relaxed, elated, and excited to sit on an old couch and gab with her younger sister.

"Yeah," I say, biting my lip to hold back tears. "I'm not going anywhere."

CHAPTER 10

MYLO

*I*t takes about ninety minutes to drive from Sudbury to the Kearsarge Hotel and Resort where Nate's wedding is being held, and to my surprise, Samantha holds my hand the entire way. She lets out a deep exhale every so often, making me think she is quite nervous about seeing her ex-husband and his family. Her brother, Marty, has offered to drive us there, so we sit in the back seat together, her small fingers tightly entwined with mine.

Marty was not pleased to sit alone in the front of the car, but Samantha immediately told him to "get fucked" and that he should be grateful she's attending at all.

The bond she shares with her brother seems somewhat volatile. They go from yelling at each other one minute to giggling about an inside joke the next. But the way he eyes me suspiciously in the rearview mirror each time he catches me staring at her legs tells me he's protective of his older sister, and that pleases me greatly. The more people Samantha has in her life to lift her and keep her safe, the better.

We arrive shortly before dusk, grabbing the keys to our rooms and dropping our bags before heading to the ceremony area. I made sure Marty's room was on the opposite end of the hall from ours, so he could not hear us…enjoying ourselves later on.

We take our seats in the very back row of white chairs, and Sam remains stiff and anxious throughout the ceremony, which drags on for much longer than feels necessary. Luckily, it takes place outdoors, and the sounds of nature buzzing in the trees paired with the spectacular view of the rocky cliff face are enough to occupy my attention.

"Seriously?" Samantha scoffs when the ceremony ends, and we get in line for drinks during cocktail hour. "A cash bar."

There is a bar inside the building where the majority of the reception is being held, as well as one outside for those who wish to drink and play lawn games in the vast patch of grass below. Inside, there is a DJ and a large dance floor in the center of the room, surrounded by several round tables adorned in crisp white tablecloths, gold napkins and flatware, and bursts of magenta in the centerpiece flowers with neatly tied bows around the vases.

"Is this not customary?" I ask. I have seen several weddings on television, but this is the first big wedding I have attended. Luka and Harper's wedding was lovely, but it was just me, my brothers, and Harper, so there was no need for a bar.

"It's cheap," she says, shaking her head. "But Nate's always been cheap."

I look around at the venue and out the many large windows at the lush, manicured landscapes, the hundreds of twinkly lights strung up in the trees, and the breathtaking view of the mountainside behind us. "This does not seem like an inexpensive place to wed."

"Oh, it's not," Marty says, rocking back on his heels as he takes in the view.

"Yeah," Samantha agrees, her scowl deepening. "He splurged on the venue but is making his guests pay for the booze. That tracks."

She is in quite a sour mood, it seems. I hold her gaze as I try to determine how to lift her spirits. That seems to pull a smile forward. "Sorry," she says, rubbing her forehead, "I don't mean to be a dick. I'm just tired."

I place my hand on her lower back and lightly rub a thumb up and down her spine. "You have not been sleeping well?" This surprises me, given that she has canceled our secret sex meetups every night this week because she was tired. I assumed she was catching up on her sleep, not losing more of it.

Samantha shakes her head. "It's fine, really. I'm fine. I just need to get a drink in me, and we can start enjoying this night."

That does seem to work. Samantha downs two gin and tonics in a matter of minutes and urges me to keep up. I pull her close. "Alcohol does not affect me the same way. I will need to consume much more to feel the same as you."

At the bar, she orders four shots of tequila, takes one for herself, and pushes the other three into my hands. "Then get to it, Marco."

I cannot help but laugh at her eagerness to see me buzzed. "As you wish, Sidney." The taste is terrible, and my throat burns after each gulp. Why do humans choose to drink such acrid swill?

Marty spends most of the reception by our side at our designated table in the far back of the room but wanders off on his own whenever Samantha and I huddle close together. Her focus is entirely on me, and her hands never seem to leave my body. They encircle my arm as she leans her head on my shoulder, wrap around my neck when we dance, and the rest of the time, her fingers thread through mine as if she is nothing but proud to have me as her date.

The feeling is mutual. I love being able to touch her freely. She doesn't protest when I pull her onto my lap and feed her steak and potatoes from my plate.

"I have my own dinner, you know," she says, wiping the corner of her mouth.

"But you need your strength for later."

She giggles as she playfully pokes me in the ribs.

"You honor me," I whisper, pressing a kiss to her brow as we sit at the table, watching as the other guests dance, eat, and drink around us.

She draws back to look at me. "How so?"

"By allowing me to be your pretend boyfriend. I must say, I enjoy the role."

Samantha tilts her head as she caresses my face, her fingertips featherlight as they trace the slope of my nose, my jaw, and over my cheeks. I've been hard since the moment I laid eyes on her in that silky purple dress that hugs her body, and now the tightness of my pants is becoming extremely uncomfortable.

"You're a natural," she says quietly before her lips descend upon mine. The kiss is quick but filled with hunger and promises of what is to come.

Marty returns with three tall glasses filled with a dark brown liquid. "Long Island iced tea," he says as he places them in front of us and sits down next to me. "The best bang for your buck at a cash bar." His gaze lingers on me as I take my glass, and just before I take a sip, he leans over and whispers, "You hurt her and I'll take a baseball bat to your skull, book boy."

I find the threat quite precious, coming from this frail human male. But he doesn't know what I truly am, and in his eyes, I'm merely a stranger who has the power to hurt his sister. My respect for Marty grows from the size of a tiny sapling into that of an ancient oak.

"Ugh, I hate these," Samantha says with a dramatic pout before taking a big sip through her bright pink straw. When the song changes, she sucks in a breath and jumps to her feet. "Oh my god, I love this song. And it's the Tiesto remix, even better." She grabs my hand and pulls me onto the dance floor.

The song seems to be about dancing alone, from the few lyrics I pick up, and alternates between lively and slow, which makes it difficult to dance to, oddly enough. Though Samantha seems to have no trouble keeping up. When it's fast, she twirls in front of me, her hips swaying side to side in a hypnotic way that leaves me breathless. When it slows, she presses her body flush against mine and rests her hands on the back of my neck as we move together.

My hands roam over her curves, and she gasps when I give the lower part of her stomach an affectionate squeeze. "What was that?" she asks, her mouth still gaping at me.

"What? Am I not allowed to touch you there?"

She blinks several times as she considers this. "Well, no, I guess it's fine. It just caught me off guard." Her brow furrows as she searches my face. I don't know what she's looking for, but she looks confused. "Why did you do that?"

I shrug. "I love that part of you, so I squeezed it. Just as I squeeze your ass," I explain, letting my hands drift down to palm the soft globes, "because I love the feel of it."

"Oh," she mutters.

Panic knots my stomach. "Did you not like it? I won't do it ag–"

"No," she says quickly, "I liked it. I definitely liked it, it's just…no one has ever done that. Grabbed my stomach in a loving way."

I move my hands back to her stomach and squeeze it again. "Shall I make up for lost time, then?"

She giggles and melts into me as the song slows even further at the end. The tip of her nose brushes against mine. "Yes, please."

We hunker down at the table for a while and enjoy the view of people dancing around us.

"There's Nate," Samantha says as her ex wanders near us, caught up in what seems to be a tense exchange with the older man who walked his new bride, Fiona, down the aisle during the ceremony. Nate gestures toward us as he struggles to say something in Spanish, and Samantha jerks back in response. "The fuck?"

Nate guides the man over to our table, and he says, "These are my friends, Marty, Sam, and uh…" He leans in as he looks at me. "Sorry, what is your name again?"

"Mylo."

"Right, this is Sam's friend, Mylo."

The man gives us a half-smile before grumbling about something under his breath and walking away. Samantha quickly scans the room, her eyes wide as she comes to a realization. "Christ on a cracker," she grabs Marty's arm, "are we the only other brown people here? Besides the bride and her family?"

"What? No," Marty scoffs. Though he was quick to dismiss the theory, as he glances around at the hundred-plus pale-faced guests, his expression tightens.

"We are," Samantha concludes. "That's why he invited me. It had nothing to do with gaining the upper hand or whatever. He wanted to look good in front of her family."

Marty scoffs. "Come on. Nate wouldn't do that."

"Nathan," Samantha shouts as she gets to her feet. The groom approaches, looking slightly nervous as he takes in her aggressive energy and her moderately drunken state.

"Sam, great to see you," he says with a tight smile. "Thank you for coming."

She cuts him off before he can continue with the pleasantries. "I'm going to ask you a question, and I want you to tell me the truth."

He chews on the inside of his cheek. "Okay…"

"Are we your token brown friends tonight?"

His mouth falls open. "Sam, how can you even ask me that?"

She stares at him for what feels like several minutes and asks again.

He doesn't budge at first. But when she says, "Are we?" a third time, his resolve evaporates, and he sighs heavily. "Okay, fine."

"Seriously, dude?" Marty asks, offended.

"Well, not you," he says to Marty. Then turns back to Sam. "But fine. I invited you so Marty didn't look like my only Hispanic friend, okay?" He rubs a circle into his temple. "Look, Fiona's dad isn't psyched about her marrying a white guy, so I thought if both of you were here, and he saw that my circle isn't made up of a bunch of white people, he might feel a little better about things."

I expect Sam to be deeply upset, but her expression is pleased, and her gaze is cunning. "Interesting. Okay, we'll play along," she says, jabbing a finger into Nate's chest, "if, and this is a big *if*, you tell the bartender that our drinks are free for the rest of the night."

"Are you serious? I'm not doing that."

Samantha shrugs as she strolls over to her seat next to me and grabs her sparkly gold clutch. "You know what? I'm actually pretty beat." She lets out a deep fake yawn and turns to Marty. "Maybe we should call it a night. Get a good night's sleep."

Marty tosses his cloth napkin onto his plate as he starts to rise. Nate looks around, panicked, and holds up his hands in surrender. "Okay, fine."

Samantha crosses her arms and waits.

"I'll go tell the bartender right now. Free drinks for the rest of the night. Just…don't leave."

Nate strolls toward the bar, and Samantha remains standing as she watches him pull the bartender aside. He points at us as he talks, and the bartender nods.

Samantha's spine straightens. "Worth it."

We continue to dance and drink for the next hour, and by the time the cake is cut, my head feels as light as air. If this is what it feels like to be drunk, I understand why humans drink so much of that foul-tasting liquid.

At some point, Samantha leans into my side and whispers, "Let's go for a walk."

I am powerless to refuse her anything, so I let her tug me toward the bar where we grab two fresh gin and tonics and head toward the back door. Before we make our escape, we pass two women who look like twins, except that the woman on the right has silver streaks throughout her hair and lines around her mouth and eyes. They are glaring at us as if we are rats trying to steal a bite of the cake.

"Sam," the younger one says as she takes a step in our direction. "You came."

Samantha's shoulders stiffen, but she keeps her smile light. "You can't be that surprised by my presence, Quinn. I did say I was coming."

Quinn. I know that name. This must be Nate's sister. Samantha warned me in the car about her and her mother, Tabitha, and how cruel they can be.

Quinn's lips flatten into a thin line. "I guess the surprise has more to do with your date than you." Quinn's eyes land on me and drift down my body in a way that makes me uncomfortable.

"Blink twice if you're not here by choice, okay? We can help you," she says to me. She cackles at her own joke, her mother joining in from where she stands a few feet away.

"I am Samantha's boyfriend, Mylo," I reply, offering them my most charming smile. "And there's no place I would rather be," I clasp Samantha's hand between both of mine, "than here with her."

Samantha stands a little taller, and I notice her muscles loosening as the tension fades. "Well, we're gonna go have sex," she proudly tells

Quinn as we head for the door. Samantha spins on her heel to face Quinn once more. "Jealousy is a disease, baby girl. Get well soon!"

We laugh as we stumble through the halls of this grand resort, Samantha carrying her strappy gold heels and her drink in one hand, the other clutching mine. I don't realize we've finished our drinks and abandoned our empty glasses until we're climbing the steps to the floor above us, and my hands are free to grip the railing.

"This way," Samantha says excitedly as we stroll down the hall, white doors with little black numbers passing by in a blur. Every floor looks the same. It would be easy to get lost inside this place.

"Ooh, what's in here?" She throws open an unmarked door to reveal a closet filled with cleaning supplies and carts filled with fresh towels. Suddenly, I'm pulled inside. Samantha slams the door behind us, and her lips are running along the length of my throat in the dark.

I groan at the feel of her tongue flicking against my earlobe. My hands travel down the elegant curve of her back, stopping to grip and squeeze the ample flesh of her ass before landing on the backs of her thighs. Lifting her into my arms, I turn her around and press her bare back into the door as I grind my hips into the apex of her thighs. She feels so good in my arms, as if she's meant to be there.

"Samantha," I growl into her neck, using my teeth to nip and tear the scrap of silk that dares to stand between my mouth and the hardened tips of her breasts.

She crosses her ankles against my lower back as she rolls her hips against me. A breathy moan escapes her lips at the friction between our bodies, and my cock throbs beneath my pants. I'm aching to the point of pain, and I want nothing more than to tear off her panties and drive into her until our bodies are sweaty and spent.

I'm able to hold her weight with one arm as I slip my other hand beneath her dress, and I've just hooked a finger around one of the flimsy straps when the door swings open, and I stagger forward, struggling to keep us both upright.

Samantha squirms in my arms until I settle her on her feet, and she quickly tugs her dress back into place. "S-sorry," we both mutter sheepishly.

The man who opened the door glares at us as he points a white-gloved finger at the closet, "You can't be in there." He looks older, possibly in his fifth decade of life, and wears a black blazer with subtle white pinstripes, matching pants, and a maroon vest.

Samantha apologizes again, and the adrenaline of being caught has us racing toward the elevators. Our chests heave once we're inside, and we burst out laughing at the awkwardness of the previous moment.

How it happens is unclear, but our lips find each other, the way they always do, and I haul Samantha into my arms, pressing her back against the wall of the elevator. The doors slide open, and she wraps her legs around me, squeezing tightly as I break into a full sprint down the hall toward our room. I slow my pace at the end of the hall, and I don't put her down as I swipe the key card and slam the door closed behind us.

She wiggles out of my grip as she pushes my suit jacket down my arms. An adorably frustrated huff leaves her lips as she attempts to loosen my tie, and I relieve her of this task by untying it myself.

We don't make it to the bed and instead become a mass of limbs on the floor in the center of the room. At some point, though, something shifts, and our pace slows way down. I spend more time tasting her skin, and I revel in the way her touch lingers on each part of mine. It feels natural to savor each other this way despite neither of us communicating a desire to linger.

I end up on my back with her straddling me, the short pile and rough texture of the carpet scraping my skin. The silky fabric of Samantha's dress ends up under my head, and as I push it away, I notice the full-length mirror directly behind me.

Samantha sinks down on my cock until our hips meet, and I become entranced by the view of her in the reflection, her breasts bouncing each time she impales herself on my length. Lifting my hips, I meet her halfway, her mouth falling open and her belly jiggling with each thrust.

"Look at yourself, Samantha," I rasp, pointing to the mirror. "Look how beautiful you are."

Her eyes widen when she notices her reflection, and I notice the instinctual movement of her hands to cover her body from even her own eyes.

Before I reach for her hands to pull them away, she drops them to my chest, and I notice the way her mouth curves up on one side as she admires her naked body. Leaning forward, she keeps her gaze on the mirror as she rolls her hips, the new angle causing my sac to tighten against my body. If she keeps this up, I'll be coming in seconds.

Her fingernails bite into my chest as she sets a slow pace. But the lack of speed isn't remotely a problem. Each time the walls of her hot cunt clench around me, the pleasure mounts at the base of my spine.

I reach up, squeezing and rolling her nipples between my fingers, and she throws her head back with a loud, keening cry.

"Samantha," I growl, "keep your eyes open." I don't want her to miss this. I want her to see what I'm seeing. "Watch yourself come." She follows my command, keeping her gaze locked on her reflection as she bounces up and down on my cock, her expression pained as her pace turns erratic.

I reach a hand between us, pressing my thumb into the side of her clit, and she comes, the wild jerking of her body creating friction that sends me careening over the edge. She collapses on top of me, her delicious body sweaty and spent as my come fills her.

Even after our chests stop heaving, something feels different. I hold her close as she presses lazy kisses all over my chest, and I can't stop my hand from running up and down her spine. There is a deep, visceral need pulsing through me to keep her right where she is for as long as she'll let me.

Is this…

Is this what making love feels like?

Refusing to chase that thought, I keep her in my grasp as I haul both of our bodies onto the large plush bed.

Samantha curls herself around my body, her leg draped over mine. I stroke her back as she snuggles against my chest, her hot breath fanning across my nipples. We spend most of the night like this, just lying together, our bodies never separating, as we talk about everything and nothing.

"Thank you for tonight," she says, lifting her head to meet my gaze. "You were the perfect fake boyfriend."

I chuckle softly as I pull her in for a kiss.

She stares at my mouth, a shy expression flashing across her face. "It almost felt...real."

"And?" I ask, prodding her to continue. I sense where this conversation is going, but I need her to state her intentions clearly.

"And what?" she asks, intentionally stalling.

"How did it feel," I begin, turning on my side so can I see her face, "pretending to be mine?"

Her teeth sink into her bottom lip. "I liked it."

I prop myself up on my elbow. Samantha's chin dips as if she cannot look me in the eye. Crooking my finger beneath that rounded, perfect chin of hers, I lift it. "I liked it too."

"Is it something you'd be interested in trying? You know, for real?"

"A relationship, you mean?"

I notice her slight wince at the R-word, but when it passes, she touches my chest, and runs her finger down my stomach, tracing the outline of each abdominal muscle. "Yeah, a relationship."

I didn't realize until now how much I wanted to have this conversation. Being her secret sex friend is certainly fun but having the freedom to touch her in front of others, to kiss her whenever I wish, that would be true luxury.

"I want to take it slow, in terms of telling people," she clarifies. "And there might be days or weeks that I can't get away, depending on how Mom's doing, but if you're willing, I'd like to give this a try."

"Yes. Yes, I want to give this a try."

She squeals happily as she rolls on top of me, peppering my face and chest with kisses. I wrap my arms around her and roll again until she's on her back. The light from the lamp in the corner shines across her face, and it's then that I notice the dark circles beneath her eyes. Despite how full of joy she is, there is crippling exhaustion just beneath the surface.

I pull her into my arms and return her head to my chest. "Do you want to sleep?" I ask, eager to continue lying here chatting with her, but content to listen to the sound of her breathing as she sleeps too.

"Not yet," she says, resting her hand on my stomach.

Moments pass as I play with her curls, coiling them around my fingers and inhaling the rich, warm scent of her perfume.

"I hope Mom goes peacefully," she says suddenly.

This is new. In the past, when I've inquired about her mother, she is quick to change the subject. I accepted that and assumed that being with me was an escape from the tragedy unfolding in front of her at home. Though, I suppose, now that I am her boyfriend, she feels more comfortable sharing the pain that fills her heart.

"I know that's not how Alzheimer's works. I've read all the books, well, audiobooks," she clarifies, "and I know that the end of this road is an onslaught of misery, but I can't imagine her spending her last days unable to get out of bed," a tear hits my skin, followed by another, and another, "or unable to speak, or swallow her food on her own. No one deserves to die like that."

"It's okay," I whisper, holding her tighter. I am aware that there's nothing okay about this situation, but there are no words to provide the comfort she seeks. So I promise her that all will be well as I massage her scalp, hoping that the warmth and security of my embrace will ease even a fraction of her suffering.

"She's…" Samantha's body trembles as her sobs quicken her breaths, making it harder for her to speak. "S-she's withering away. Right in front of me." She sniffles as she swipes the back of her hand across her face. "There's n-nothing I can do to stop it."

"I am here," I offer, hating that I cannot fix this problem for her. "It's okay."

Eventually, her sniffles cease, and the tears on my stomach dry. She falls asleep with her head on my chest, and her adorably loud snores tell me this might be the most restful slumber she's had in far too long.

As her official boyfriend, I decide it is my duty to make sure she gets enough rest from this day forward, even if that means coming to her house to read to Elena while she naps. At some point, I nod off, too, and awaken when the sun is high in the sky to the loud, erratic thumps of a fist against the door.

Passing the full-length mirror, I'm reminded to mask myself, and I do so before opening the door to find Marty, his eyes bloodshot and his hair mussed as he holds his phone in his hand.

"Marty?" Samantha asks, sitting up in bed and wrapping the sheets around her chest. "What is it?"

"Mom," he croaks. His eyes fill with tears. "She's in the hospital."

CHAPTER 11

SAM

I sit in the front with Marty as he races down I-93 South, going well over the speed limit. He's shaky, and I need him focused so that we make it to Mom's bedside in one piece. Once he burst into our room, he broke down as he relayed the information Jackie gave him, but I couldn't understand half of what he told us beyond "fell" and "stairs." I tried calling Jackie, but she didn't answer. I assume she's dealing with the doctors in charge of Mom's care.

"Tell me again," I say to Marty. "What, exactly, did Jackie say happened?"

Marty takes a few deep breaths, wiping away the tears that continue to fall down his cheeks. "Um, she called me from the ambulance and said that she was asleep on the couch and woke up to Mom wandering around the upstairs hallway in the dark, and that Mom fell down the stairs before she could get a word out to warn her."

I try calling Jackie again, and this time, she picks up. "Sam, oh my god, it's bad," she says through muffled cries.

"Tell me what's happening."

"I don't know," she cries. "There's swelling in the brain. Sam, there was s-so much blood."

Her breathing turns shallow, and the sound of hiccups meets my ears, making it even harder to understand her. I try to keep my frustration in check, but I have no idea what's going on, and it seems like she can't form a full sentence. "But she's alive? Jackie, is she alive?"

"Yeah," she says, then hands the phone to her husband, Dan.

"Hey, Sam," he says in a somber tone. He doesn't wait for me to ask, he just starts talking, which I'm grateful for. "She's in an induced coma. Apparently, she hit her head pretty hard, and there's swelling in the brain. She also has a fractured hip, and a few cracked ribs," he pulls the phone away to ask Jackie, "Was it two or three cracked ribs?"

I can't hear Jackie, but Dan says, "Right," then adds, "two cracked ribs."

He says they're taking her into surgery to repair the hip in the next half hour, and where to go once we arrive. I relay this to Marty and Mylo after Dan hangs up, and silence fills the car for the next hour.

I expect to cry, but the tears don't come. There are so many unknowns that I don't feel sad, just terrified of what's coming. Will she make it through surgery? Or will she succumb to her injuries before she even wakes up?

Marty doesn't say it, but I wonder if he's thinking about the baby gate right now. He suggested we install one to prevent this very thing from happening, and I urged him not to because it wasn't worth upsetting her.

There's gonna come a day when we'll have to put her safety above her happiness.

That day came too late, and it's all my fault.

Mom's still in surgery when we arrive at Concord Hospital, and it's just Jackie waiting there for us. "Where's Dan?" I ask.

"He went to Mom's house to clean up."

"Clean up?"

Her eyes fill with tears. "The blood, Sammy." She ducks her head into my chest as sobs overtake her. "So much blood."

I look at Marty, silently pleading for help. He gently extracts Jackie from my front and pulls her in for a hug. She goes willingly, and I look for the nearest nurse or doctor. Then, one of the last faces I ever wanted to see again is the first one that comes into view. "Beth," I mutter, wondering what I did in a past life to deserve such rotten luck, "you're a nurse?"

She nods as she fiddles with a chart in her hands. "Sure am. Front-line pandemic hero." She looks me up and down. "You still taking your little pictures?"

I haven't seen her since the reunion. What a terrible night that was. She and Vanessa confronted each other in the bathroom, and Beth made sure to make a heartless comment about my mom's disease before she left. The night ended with the death of her boyfriend, Trevor, the man who raped both me and Vanessa.

I can't speak for Vanessa, but I wake up every day feeling grateful Trevor no longer roams this Earth, and any grief Beth still feels, well, she's an asshole, so I'm not concerned about her feelings.

Although, I might have to be nice to her if... "You're not my mom's nurse, are you?"

Please say no. Please say no.

"No, I'm working the neonatal unit today."

Phew, thank you, Jesus. Though I feel bad for those babies. Their little bodies working so hard to survive, and they're greeted with the angular sneer of this bitch? That's a rough start.

"What's going on with your mom?" she asks. I can tell she's not genuinely interested by the slight smirk she's failing to hide. She wants gossip, and even more, she wants to see me crack.

Not going to happen.

"Why am I even talking to you?" I ask, shoving past her toward the doctor coming down the hall. My mom is in a fucking coma. I can't waste my time on Beth of all people.

I tell him why I'm here, and who I'm here for.

"She's probably still in surgery," he assures me. "That's typically a three-hour procedure. Wait here. Take a seat. Get comfortable. I'll make sure your mother's surgeon updates you as soon as possible."

The four of us, Jackie, Marty, me, and Mylo, settle into a quiet corner of the waiting room. Jackie cries as Marty comforts her, then they trade off as Marty starts to cry. I can't sit still, so I step away from the group and pace up and down the long, brightly lit hallway as my head pounds from an excess of booze and lack of water.

I should be exhausted right now, given how little sleep I've had this week, but the adrenaline from the news of Mom's fall continues pumping through my blood, making it impossible for me to sit and wait.

Mylo paces with me, staying quiet and remaining by my side, and as thankful as I am for his presence, it feels like hovering, and I can't handle that right now. When I stop walking, he does too, and we lean heavily against the wall, side by side.

"I wish there was something I could do," he says, looking down at the floor.

"Yeah, me too," I reply, not knowing what else to say, and I don't exactly feel compelled to fill the silence. Silence means there's no news, and no news means that Mom is okay. Because if she weren't, they'd come out and tell us. There would be words laced with sorrow followed by the loud, undignified sobs of me and my siblings. Yes, silence is where hope lives.

Mylo clearly doesn't feel the same because he keeps trying to offer me words of comfort that feel hollow, not because he doesn't mean them, I'm certain that he does, but until I know Mom is going to survive this, telling me that "everything will be okay" seems pointless. He doesn't know that everything will be okay, and I don't need him to feed me empty promises.

"Look at it this way," he begins, and my teeth grind at how little I want to engage, "if your mother dies in surgery, you will not have to witness her suffering."

It takes a second for the words to register. When they do, I instinctively put distance between us. "What did you just say?"

He doesn't seem to notice the shift in my mood, so he digs in deeper. "I mean that if she never awakens, her death will have been quick, which means her suffering was minimal. That's a good thing, is it not?"

"I-I'm sorry," I stammer, "I'm not ready to...I'm not going to consider that yet."

He looks confused. "But you said last night that you did not want to watch her wither away. If she dies today, you will have avoided that. Her mind has not turned to mush. Not yet. And you will be able to remember the woman that she was before, right?"

If she dies today and *mush* are the words I latch onto, and I feel my heart race as they play over and over again in my head. I can't believe he would say that to me. Especially in the waiting room while she's in surgery to have her fractured hip repaired and her brain swells inside her skull. What did he think telling me that would accomplish? Did he truly believe it would cheer me up to think of her dying here in a hospital instead of at home?

I can tell the moment he realizes he's fucked up because he starts fidgeting with the folded cuffs of his dress shirt. "Samantha, I did not mean it in a bad way."

"Oh, you didn't mean it in a bad way?" I repeat, rolling my eyes. "Just because I don't want to see her suffer doesn't mean I want her to die today. Okay? I don't want either outcome."

He considers this, then tilts his head and gives me a look like he's not done digging this hole. "But surely you realize that one of the two outcomes is likely to occur."

Why is he doing this? Why is he trying to infuse logic into this moment? "I don't care," I bark out, my patience gone completely. "I don't...I—can you just leave me the fuck alone, please?" It came out louder than I wanted it to, and now everyone in the waiting room is staring at us.

His face falls, and guilt twists my stomach. I didn't mean to yell at him; I just can't hear him list the reasons why my mom's potential sudden death would be a positive thing. It doesn't matter if his intentions were good when he started talking. His words have sliced through me, and now I can't picture anything but her lifeless body inside a coffin.

"May I see you tonight?" he asks quietly, reaching for my hand.

I yank it away. "I don't know." Then I consider what recovery for this type of injury might look like. "No, I'm going to stay here until they say she can go home."

He steps closer, shoving his hands in his pockets instead of reaching for me again. "Samantha, I am your boyfriend now. Don't retreat. Let me in."

"I can't do this right now," I tell him. My gaze drifts to Jackie and Marty. I can't bring myself to look at Mylo right now. I know this will hurt him, but I don't have the energy to prioritize his emotional needs over my mom who is barely clinging to life.

"*This*, as in this conversation? Or this relationship? Which of those can you not do?"

I let out a reluctant sigh. "Both." Mom needs me here. Mylo will be fine.

He opens his mouth, obviously about to protest, when I whisper, "It's not like your eyes have turned red for me. This was just a fun fling. We're not meant to be." I hate saying the words, but it's not as if they're untrue. If I were his mate, wouldn't we both know by now?

The fact that his eyes are still that deep gray with flecks of gold means his mate is still out there. And what happens when they meet? If we were still together when that happened, he'd choose her in an instant, and I'd be left behind with my heart broken.

Besides, I didn't want to get attached to him in the first place. I should never have asked him to that wedding. Then I wouldn't know what it feels like to be his. I'd have no idea how it feels to be held in his arms in the middle of a crowded dance floor, with every woman's eyes on him while his eyes remain on me—gazing at me like I'm the only star in the sky.

A muscle in his jaw ticks as he nods somberly. "Very well. I shall go."

I want to hug him and tell him I'm sorry, but I'm not sure what I'd be apologizing for. He shouldn't have said what he said even if he was trying to make me feel better. He's been on this planet long enough to know better.

Even if he hadn't said those things, my mom has a long road to recovery after that fall. I doubt I'll have enough free time for a relationship anyway.

I watch him leave until he turns a corner and disappears from sight, leaving me alone with my thoughts. Those thoughts center around that damn baby gate, and how having it installed would've prevented this entire nightmarish mess.

CHAPTER 12

SAM

*O*nce Mom's procedure is over, and her vitals remain stable, the doctor tells us the surgery was a success, but stresses that she's not out of the woods yet. The swelling in her brain needs to go down, and that could take days.

I spend the next twenty-four hours in the dress I wore to Nate's wedding, dozing on and off in the chair next to Mom's bed until Jackie returns to the hospital with a change of clothes she picked up at the house. "I'm so glad Dan cleaned the stairs. Didn't prevent me from breaking down the moment I opened the door, though," she says with a deprecating smirk and a sniffle. "Here, go change." She hands me the bag, containing fresh underwear, socks, a pair of baggy sweatpants, and an oversized T-shirt. "You look like a prom queen that got lost in the woods and found twenty years later."

I chuckle as I walk barefoot across Mom's hospital room and into the small adjoining bathroom.

"There's deodorant in there too," Jackie notes. "Do us all a favor and put some on, will you?"

I come back out a few minutes later and stay standing. I feel like I've been sitting for an eternity. My body wants to move, so I allow it to pace. Jackie yawns as she takes my chair. "When did Marty leave?" she asks.

"A couple hours ago."

"You sure you don't want to go home for a bit and get some sleep? I can stay with Mom today."

"No," I tell her. I haven't left the hospital since we got here, and I don't plan on leaving until Mom's ready to go home with me. "I'm good."

I feel Jackie's eyes on me, and eventually, she asks, "Everything okay with you and the hunky librarian?"

Where do I even begin? We broke up, so no, we're not okay, but before that happened, we had an amazing night together. Probably one of the best nights of my life. Can this thing between us be salvaged? I don't know. "Not really" is all I say because I'm too tired to get into the details, and these chairs are nowhere near comfortable enough to sleep on. "I don't want to talk about it."

She nods. "Fair enough."

We listen to the steady beep of Mom's heart monitor, intentionally not addressing the elephant in the room. I want to ask what she thinks will happen to Mom, but I'm not ready for another depressingly negative response, so I remain quiet. She does the same.

By day three, the swelling in Mom's brain still has not gone down despite the many tubes attached to her and the many beeping machines connected to said tubes. Marty and Jackie have created a routine around their visits, where Jackie comes first thing in the morning and stays until Marty arrives in the afternoon. There's an overlap of about an hour when the three of us are together, and Marty stays into the night until he gets tired.

Holly and Dan have come by several times to deliver flowers for Mom or snacks for us, and it makes me tempted to text Mylo to see if we can start again after all this is over and Mom is home. But ultimately, I decide against it before I reach for my phone. It's better to wait until I know Mom will be okay before promising any of my time to fix what's broken.

Marty arrives around three in the afternoon, just as a nurse comes in to pull more blood from Mom's arm. She's had a slight fever since yesterday morning, and they're worried about an infection. The doctor on duty comes in and tells us they're switching her to a different antibiotic because the one they put her on yesterday doesn't seem to be working.

"Okay, and this one will work?" Marty asks the doctor, whose name tag says Dr. Walsh.

"We can't say for sure, but we're hoping it will," she replies.

Typical doctor. I haven't gotten a straight answer from any of them since we got here. I know they can't make any promises, but it would be nice to see some confidence from someone in charge of keeping my mother alive.

"What about the swelling in her brain?" I ask. This is my main concern. Antibiotics fight infections. That's their job. But are we really living in a time when the medical response to a swollen brain is "let's wait and see?" Waiting and seeing never saved anybody.

"I can assure you, Miss Rodriguez, we're doing all that we can to decrease the swelling," she explains patiently. "Oxygen therapy, the medications we have her on, and the IV are all working together to accomplish this. We just need to wait for the brain to respond."

Why isn't there a surgical procedure, or, like, a fucking laser that can reduce swelling in the brain? What they're doing now isn't working quickly enough. What if it stays swollen and causes brain damage? What if she loses her sight or her ability to walk? What if—

The doctor reaches her hand out and places it on my shoulder, and my anxious train of thought slows enough for me to catch my breath. "I know the waiting is the worst part. But this is out of your control. For now, there's nothing left to do but wait."

I don't like that answer, but it seems pointless to argue, so I pull up a chair and hold my head in my hands as the doctor leaves. Marty goes back to playing games on his phone while Jackie reopens the book she brought. And we wait.

I haven't checked my phone since we arrived at the hospital days ago, and as bored as I am just sitting here, I also have no interest in updating anybody on Mom's status. Particularly since it feels like we still don't have enough information.

Will she be okay?

When will she be released?

Are you okay?

I don't have answers to those questions, and I'm unable to fake positivity right now and say that everything will be fine, even via text.

For the first time since I was ten years old, I pray. I don't do it aloud because I'm certain Marty and Jackie would give me shit, but I know Mom would appreciate it. She was still lighting a candle every time she lost something until the frequency of that became a fire hazard. Her church friends stop by once a week to check on her, and her rosary beads are always on her nightstand.

So for her, I send a silent plea to God to bring my mother back. To give her more time.

Hours pass, and Jackie stays. I'm not sure why, but I'm glad about it. I need her and Marty here right now. Mom does too. I offer to get us all coffees from the little cart down the hall, and Marty and Jackie reply with matching smiles—smiles I haven't seen in days.

Just as I'm adding sugar to Marty's cup, I hear a commotion coming from down the hall. I turn to see a doctor and two nurses racing into Mom's room, and Marty and Jackie being pushed out. The coffee in my hand falls to the floor, the hot brown liquid splattering over the immaculately clean tile, and I run toward my siblings as my heart sinks.

"What, what, what?" I shout when I reach their side. "What's happening?"

Jackie sobs as she leans into Marty's chest, and his skin turns so pale, I worry he's about to pass out. "I-I don't know," he says, trying to swallow back tears of his own. "Her machines started beeping louder and, and, and when the nurse came in, she said something about blood pressure dropping, and I don't...I don't know."

One of the nurses must've shut the door because it's now closed, and I can't hear what's going on inside beyond a flurry of activity.

I wrap my arms around both of them, but the tears still don't come.

I'm too scared. Numb with fear. Frozen in place. I just keep holding onto them as if they're my source of oxygen.

"We'll wait," I say with a sardonic chuckle. "We'll just wait."

But we don't have to wait long. The doctor emerges from the room first, wearing the kind of stoic expression I'm sure took her years to master, yet the grim line of her mouth gives her away.

"Passed."

"...so sorry."

Jackie folds in on herself, her knees smacking into the floor as she lets out a gut-wrenching cry. Marty starts hyperventilating when the doctor utters the words "likely sepsis."

My hands somehow remain connected to both of them as they react to the news, my right on Jackie's shoulder, and my left on Marty's arm as the hallway takes on a strange fuzzy quality. The doctor is still standing there, but I can't hear what she's saying. All I hear is the dull ringing in my ears, and the throbbing pain behind my left eye grows louder by the second.

I don't know if I say anything, or if I cry, or scream upon learning that my mother is gone. It's as if I'm trapped in a giant fish tank, suspended in water, my surroundings blurred and muffled.

Minutes stop passing in a linear sense after that, and time itself becomes a collection of fragments, some of note, but most insignificant. Mom's machines are disconnected. Jackie calls Dan. Marty empties his water bottle and angrily hurls it across the room, the plastic bouncing off the wall and rolling across the floor. Eventually, Mom's body is wheeled out. A nurse comes in and I hear "arrangements" mentioned to Jackie.

I'm not sure how long the three of us sit there in heavy silence or how long we're allowed to stay, but no one comes in to kick us out.

At some point, Jackie asks, "How long was she sleepwalking?"

I press the heel of my palm against my left eye, trying to stop the throb. "What?"

"Mom. How long was she sleepwalking?" she asks again. "I didn't see it in the notebook."

"That's because I didn't write it in the notebook," I tell her in a flat tone.

Her eyebrows lift as she rolls her eyes. "Of course not," she mutters under her breath.

"Why would I write it in the notebook when I can just tell you it happened?" I say, not in the mood to discuss the pros and cons of my sister's many rules. "No one writes in the notebook but you."

"Well, maybe you should have," she snaps. "If I had known she was sleepwalking, maybe I could've done something."

I gesture to Marty. "Marty knew about it. I told him days ago."

Marty's gaze drops to the floor.

"That notebook was for all of us," Jackie spits. "It was to help us stay on top of how the disease was affecting her and track the progression. Would it have really been so hard for you guys to jot down your thoughts at the end of the day?" Her eyes are like daggers as they shift between me and Marty. "Or, I don't know, read anything that I wrote down?"

"I added stuff to the notebook," Marty notes, sheepishly.

Nope. Not letting him get away with this one. "Your fucking doodles don't count."

The vein in Jackie's neck is starting to show, a clear indication of how close she is to losing her shit. "Maybe if you had read even one word in the notebook, Sam, just one fucking word, then you wouldn't have let her watch *Real Housewives,* or let her eat sodium-filled garbage, or, or allowed her to get so dehydrated that she roams around the house in the middle of the night, not knowing where the hell she is."

"Are you suggesting that dehydration is the reason she fell, and that I'm the cause of her dehydration? Like I was callously withholding water from her?"

She shrugs. "All I'm saying is that dehydration causes confusion, and clearly she was confused when she fell."

I don't feel myself rising from my chair until I'm on my feet and looking down at Jackie. "Oh, is that all you're saying? Really? Why not sprinkle in some subtext for the class, huh? Why not just say what it is you're obviously thinking?"

She crosses her arms and leans back in her chair. "Yeah? And what is it that I'm obviously thinking?"

I spread my arms out wide, ready for her barrage of verbal bullets. "Uh, that I killed Mom."

"I never said that."

"I said you were thinking it."

"And you know what I'm thinking?"

"Enough!" Marty yells. His face is red and tear-streaked, and his lips are peeled back, exposing his teeth in a rage-filled expression that makes him look feral. He rubs his nose with the back of his hand, and his chest heaves as he looks between Jackie and me. "This is the kind of shit that rips a family apart. This, right here."

He grabs his wallet and phone off the circular side table and heads for the door. "I'm going home." Marty turns to face us as he holds the door open with his foot. "You're not going to forget what is said today, on the day of Mom's..." his bottom lip trembles as he's unable to finish his sentence. "Choose your words carefully."

Not another word passes between Jackie and me, not even when we leave the hospital, and she drives me home. And not even when I get out of the car.

My thoughts are loud enough. Like a megaphone inside my head, "Baby gate!" "Dehydration!" and "Sepsis!" blare at the highest volume as if coming from a tiny cheerleading squad buried deep inside my brain tissue, waving their pom-poms and reminding me that Mom's death is entirely on me.

I did this. She's dead because of me.

As I stop halfway up the stairs, I notice a small spot of blood that Dan must've missed. The sight of it sends me to my knees, and my entire body shakes with the force of my sobs. It doesn't matter how hard I scrub that wall. The memory of what happened here will always remain.

"Mom," I cry out to no one as I inch back down the stairs. "Mom." At some point, darkness creeps in through the corners of my vision, and I picture her face, hoping she's about to take me with her.

CHAPTER 13

MYLO

*I*t has been over a week since I saw Samantha at the hospital. I had hoped our reunion would take place under happier circumstances, but today is her mother's funeral, and even though we have not spoken, and I have no idea where we stand, I'm going to be there for her.

Zev and I ride to the church in Kyan's Mercedes SUV while Axil and Vanessa follow us in his truck. The church is crowded when we arrive, and I spot Samantha at the front pew flanked by Jackie and Jackie's husband, Dan, I think his name is. Two young boys encircle Jackie, one tugging on her hand, and one wrapped around her leg. Samantha's expression is stoic, which does not surprise me. The walls around her heart are up, surrounded by a moat filled with sharks.

She may think she's made of steel, but I see the cracks in her armor, the dark circles beneath her eyes, the pallid shade of her otherwise glowing complexion, and the flatness of her curls. Samantha is struggling.

"I'm going to go see her, okay?" Vanessa says to Axil. "I'll be right back."

Once she's out of earshot, Axil leans toward me. "Are you well, brother?"

I shrug.

The sex friendship Samantha and I had is no longer a secret. Nor is the fact that we began a very short-lived relationship. On the way from the hotel to the hospital, I texted my brothers to let them know what happened, as I was not sure how long I'd be by Samantha's side.

By the time I left the hospital and came home, Samantha was no longer my girlfriend, and I was upset, feeling powerless about the whole situation. I told them everything, Vanessa, too, and they've continued to check on me every day since.

After that first day, I tried brushing this off. She had a point about my eyes not changing for her. It's not as if we were together for long either. Moving on should not be difficult. But I have tried forgetting her. I've tried turning my focus to my work. There is certainly plenty to do with the upcoming fundraisers I've planned and the recent graffiti that was sprayed over the posters advertising Uma Sinner's story hour we had hanging in the front windows. But it's not working. Nothing has worked to remove her grip on my soul.

I think of her constantly, and my draxilio is in even worse shape. He whines day and night until I can take no more of it and let him out. The moment I shift, he takes me to her house, and he remains hovering above her roof, flapping his wings through the sticky, stifling summer air, wondering if she's all right, hoping to catch a glimpse of her until his wings grow tired and he lets me have control.

"Here," Kyan says, stopping at a pew in the middle of the church. He enters the row and takes his seat, but Zev, Axil, and I remain standing, unsure of the etiquette. Should I approach Samantha now and offer my condolences? Or wait until after the service?

Ultimately, I decide to wait. If she is doing her best to keep it together, I don't want to be the reason she crumbles.

After Vanessa returns to Axil's side, I notice a pair of elderly women approach Samantha, and her smile is tight as they speak to her. More people filter into the church, and the pews start to fill. Minutes from the official start of the service, a wheezing cough meets my ears and sends a chill down my spine.

Turning toward the source, I see Officer Burton at the back of the church, standing next to a woman who looks vaguely familiar, but I'm having trouble placing her.

Axil and Vanessa don't, though, and simultaneously groan at the sight of her. "Of course, Beth is here with that fucker," Vanessa whispers to Axil.

I'm not entirely sure what that means, but it doesn't seem like a compliment.

The moment Samantha registers their presence, I can't help but smile at the defiant, barely contained fury that flashes across her face. I can see it all playing out beforehand, but as the moment unfolds in the present, it's even sweeter to watch. She gently, but firmly nudges people out of her way as she strides down the center aisle. She stops a few feet in front of the duo and says, "Nope. Get the fuck out. Both of you."

All chatter in the church ceases immediately as heads turn in her direction. Officer Burton and Beth remain silent, somewhat taken aback by her demand.

Samantha is not deterred.

"You heard me," she says, pointing at the door. "Out."

"Miss Rodriguez, we're simply here to pay our respects," Officer Burton says in a patronizing tone.

Jackie overhears the exchange and struggles to push through the crowd. Eventually, she arrives at Samantha's side. "Everything okay over here?"

"Absolutely," Samantha says with a confident grin. "We'll be fan-fucking-tastic as soon as these two make their exit."

Officer Burton scoffs. "This doesn't seem like an appropriate tone for such a sad occasion." He looks around at the crowd that's gathering around them. "Am I right, people?"

Silence follows. After that, Samantha's wrath. "Did it seem appropriate to tell my mother to go back to her own country in front of her coworkers, Officer Burton?"

His lips part, and Samantha revels in his obvious discomfort.

"Yeah. I bet you thought I had forgotten that, huh?" When he says nothing, Samantha continues. "What about the fact that your rat-faced loser of a nephew was a known rapist, and you did nothing to hold him accountable? What about that?"

Beth's expression goes from sour to fuming at Samantha's mention of Trevor. Officer Burton stays quiet but is clearly just as incensed as Beth is.

Samantha steps forward. "Today is my mother's funeral, and I think I'm well within my rights to boot your racist ass out of here."

She looks at Beth. "Ugh, I don't have to spell it out for you, do I, Beth?" She nods toward the exit. "Just go."

The priest approaches from behind Samantha and clears his throat. "Dear, this is God's house. All are welcome."

"Not today, they're not," she replies. "At least, not during the service." Samantha turns to face them once again. "You want to come back and pray? Do it after three p.m. Until then, I get to choose who honors her memory, and neither of you are on the guest list."

Vanessa starts clapping the moment Samantha is done speaking, and it makes me realize how alone she must feel right now. These two deeply unpleasant humans attempted to crash her mother's funeral, and she is the only one refusing to allow it. I get to my feet, nodding at my brothers to follow as I exit the pew. I hear Axil grumble his caution, but I ignore it. The repercussions of what I'm about to do are nothing compared to the pain that Samantha must be feeling. And it's important that someone in this town takes a stand against Burton.

I hear Vanessa say, "Oh hell yeah," as she follows us toward the doors. We make our way through the crowd and stand next to each other in a row once we get between Samantha and Officer Burton.

"You were asked to leave," I tell Officer Burton, straightening my spine. "I suggest you do so."

He smirks as he looks from me to each of my brothers. Then he steps forward until he's mere inches away from me. "You think it's wise to threaten a police officer?" Then he whispers, "I'm armed, you know."

Kyan leans toward Burton. "I'm sure shooting mourners in a church will do wonders for your reputation."

Burton's mouth curls into a grimace and his gaze narrows on me as if silently promising that he won't forget this.

The crowd settles once he and Beth leave, and Samantha and her siblings take their place in the front pew. The priest starts speaking, but I don't pay attention to what he says. My eyes are locked on the back of Samantha's head, and my draxilio will not let me look away.

The priest invites members of the family to come up and speak, and the three siblings step up to the microphone together. Jackie stands in the middle with a sheet of paper in her shaking hands, with Marty and Samantha towering over her slight frame on either side.

Jackie thanks the crowd for coming, but when she starts reminiscing about her mother, she starts to cry. She makes several attempts to swallow her pain, but the tears continue in a steady stream down her cheeks. Marty gets choked up at the sight of his sister crying and is also unable to speak. Samantha reluctantly takes the paper Jackie hands her, and my hands flex at my sides as I watch her trying to read it.

She can't, though, and I'm not sure if anyone else in this room understands that. She looks up from the paper and swallows, then back down at the array of jumbled letters in front of her.

Go to her, my draxilio urges. *Pull her out of this moment. Read it for her.*

As much as I want to, I can't. She has already been put on the spot to read aloud in front of a large group of people at her mother's funeral, running up there and taking the paper from her would only make her secret struggle more obvious to onlookers, and that's the last thing she would want.

I remain seated, cracking my knuckles as I am forced to watch my breathtaking, passionate, strong, former sex friend try to overcome what must feel like a waking nightmare.

My anxiety dulls the moment she puts the paper on the podium. She rubs her forehead for a moment, then glances at the coffin to her right. "I, uh, I'll make this brief," she begins, her voice somewhat robotic. "Thank you all for being here. My mother…she, um, she probably would not have been thrilled by my little outburst, earlier…" Samantha chuckles, and many in the audience follow suit. Her eyes drift over the faces of the many people here, and land on one in particular, "Oh, Mrs. Davis is here. Hi."

Jackie, still crying, gently nudges Samantha's arm.

That seems to pull her focus back to the present, and she clears her throat. "I'm sure Mom would be pleased that you're all here today to celebrate her life. And the flowers," she gestures to the massive bouquet draped over the center of the coffin, "she would've loved those too." Her tone remains stiff and her eyes vacant as she continues to ramble, singling out Mrs. Davis once more to thank her for coming, then asking Jackie if she did that already.

Marty composes himself enough to pull the mic away from Samantha and add, "Mom was a force to be reckoned with. She will be missed." Then he ushers his sisters off the stage.

After the service ends, we stand in line to offer our condolences. When it's my turn, Samantha takes my hand and leans in toward my ear. "Hey, meet me in the hallway near the bathrooms in five minutes," she whispers and doesn't let go of my hand until I agree to do so.

Her request puzzles me. She has refused to return my calls and texts, and has made no effort to reach out to me since she ended our relationship, and now, suddenly, she wants to chat? I make my way through the back of the church with the rest of the mourners, into the cramped back room that has a handful of folding chairs and two long tables covered with sandwiches, individual bags of chips, and several bottles of soda and water. Through a side door, I find the hallway and lean against the wall between the bathrooms.

She finds me not long after, and without saying a word, grabs my hand and pulls me into a mop closet. Her lips brush against mine, and then they're trailing down my neck as she begins unbuttoning my shirt. Confused, and regrettably, extremely hard, I grab her hands and gently push her back, putting space between us.

"What are you doing?" I ask.

She tries stepping toward me, but I grab hold of her shoulders and keep her right where she is. "What do you think I'm doing?"

Is she truly attempting to seduce me right now? After a week of shutting me out completely? "Samantha, no."

"No?" she draws back as if slapped. "All those texts you sent, asking if there's anything you can do. Yet the moment I need you, you reject me?"

"This is how you want me to help you?"

"Yes," she says, exasperated. "Make me forget that my mom just died."

I loosen my grip on her, letting my hands drop to my sides. "No," I repeat, annoyed that a quick fuck in a closet is all I'm good for in Samantha's eyes, and disgusted with myself that I'm still hard, still desperate to taste her skin.

Her lip trembles as she wraps her arms around her middle. Seeing her pained expression knowing I put it there feels like a bullet ripping through my flesh.

"You don't want me anymore? What, is it because of my speech?"

She thinks my feelings for her would fade after one bad speech? That's absurd. She could spend the rest of her days muttering nonsensical things to large crowds and it wouldn't dampen my need for her.

"This has nothing to do with that," I tell her.

"So, what is it? I thought we were clear on what this was."

"But then you gave me a glimpse at something more." I don't understand what's so difficult about entering a relationship with me. Why isn't she willing to give this a try? I'm not asking her to be my mate.

Although, since my eyes haven't turned red, I wonder why I'm bothering to seek out her affections at all. Just because my draxilio thinks she's my mate doesn't mean she is. Unless my eyes turn red for her, she's just another human female. I should be able to resist her.

She sighs, leaning back against the shelf with several dust-covered bottles of bleach. "What if this is all I have to give?"

I don't want to say what I'm about to say. My draxilio can sense it, and he starts growling immediately. There's no other way around it, though. If I fail to establish this boundary, I will continue to feel used by her, even if that isn't her intention. Worse, I will begin to hate myself, and I refuse to go down that path. Sighing deeply, I take one last look at Samantha. "Then give it to someone else."

CHAPTER 14

SAM

Time slows as I adjust to life without Mom. She was my purpose, and caring for her took up the majority of my waking hours. Now that she's gone, I have no idea what to do with myself.

I want to sleep, but it continues to evade me. When the sun is shining, exhaustion hits like a freight train, but the moment my eyes close, I hear "Baby gate!" "Dehydration!" "Sepsis!" chanted at full volume inside my skull, and I end up staying awake until night comes when my energy tends to peak. It's totally backward, and I can't make any sense of it other than accepting this as part of the grief process, I guess, and I need to ride it out until my body shuts down.

My appetite only appears in the middle of the afternoon, which is when I tend to have takeout delivered. I don't have the desire nor the energy to cook my own meals, so I'll just do this until my money runs out, which should be soon if the alerts from my bank that keep popping up on my phone are any indication.

The couch has become my bed as it's the shortest distance to the fridge and the half-bathroom by the front door. Showering would require me to climb the stairs that killed my mother, so I've stopped taking them altogether. It's not like I have anyone to impress anyway.

It's just me in this old, empty house that suddenly feels way too big for just one person. Mom's smile lit up every room. Her laughter echoed through the hall, and if she was making her homemade *pasteles*, you could smell them from the driveway.

This house *was* Mom. Now, it's just a collection of wood and nails devoid of any joy or personality at all.

"Ugh, what the hell?" Marty mutters as he bursts through the front door and starts kicking my collection of empty pizza boxes aside. "Sam, what is all this?"

Jackie enters behind him, and her face scrunches up in disgust. "This house has been yours for three days and look at what you've done to it."

I don't have it in me to defend myself, or to fight, so I just shrug and pull the comforter from my bed up to my chin and burrow into the cushions of the couch.

Jackie drops her purse on the dining room table and makes her way to Mom's chair. She plops down and turns toward me. "We're supposed to go through Mom's things today. Did you forget?"

I search my memories, but it doesn't register. "I guess so?"

Marty and Jackie exchange a look of pity, and when Jackie nods in my direction, Marty takes the seat next to me on the couch.

"You're not okay," he says. It wasn't even a question, and I can't blame him for being so direct. He's right.

"No," I mutter, rubbing my eyes. "I'm really not." Uncomfortable with the vulnerability that threatens to rise to the surface, I brush it off with dark humor. "But, you know, Mom's dead because of me, so I should probably get used to being not okay."

They don't laugh. I don't expect them to.

Jackie leans forward, her eyes wide. "Do you truly believe that?"

She has to ask? She basically accused me of intentionally dehydrating Mom and causing her fall moments after she died. "Uh, yeah."

Jackie winces as she hunches forward, dropping her head in her hands. "That's not true, Sam. I'm sorry for making you think you were responsible for such a terrible, tragic accident."

That's nice of her to say, but it doesn't change anything. "You were right, though. I didn't read the notebook. I let her eat her favorite foods and watch *Real Housewives*. And I objected when Marty suggested installing that fucking baby gate."

Jackie doesn't offer a reply. She leans back in Mom's chair and pinches her eyes closed.

"I bought it," Marty says out of the blue.

"What?" Jackie asks.

"The baby gate. I bought it," he admits, staring intently at the corner of the bottom stair. "It was in my trunk the night of the wedding. I planned to install it the next day." His gaze lifts to each of us, but just for a second, before dropping to his feet. Then he shakes his head. "Yeah. I didn't care about your objections, Sammy. I thought it was the right thing to do." His nostrils flare, and I can see the tears that fill his eyes. "If I had installed it one day earlier. Just...just one day, then maybe..." he trails off, covering his eyes.

I reach for his hand, and he lets me take it.

Jackie sighs heavily. "I saw Mom sleepwalking a few weeks ago, and I didn't put it in the notebook." Her voice is shaky as she continues. "When I noticed you guys weren't writing in it, I stopped writing in it too." She chuckles softly. "I guess it was my stupid, petty way of punishing you. Like, if you weren't going to share your observations, then I wasn't going to either. Which is ridiculous, I know. How would that even be a form of punishment when you didn't read it to begin with?"

I lean over the arm of the couch and take her hand. She nods as she looks down at where our hands are joined, and a slight smile tugs at her lips. This was hard for her to admit, and I want her to know I'm listening.

"I really meant to tell you about the sleepwalking. It's not like I wanted you to be in the dark about what was happening with Mom. I just kept forgetting."

"You should've written it down," Marty adds with a smirk, sending all three of us into a welcomed fit of laughter.

When our laughter fades, I squeeze both of their hands. "I'm dyslexic. I didn't read the notebook because I can't." I lock eyes with Jackie. "Your handwriting is atrocious."

She doesn't laugh at my joke. Instead, she takes my hand in both of hers and shakes her head. "Why didn't you tell me? Tell us. My god, Sam. How long have you been struggling with this on your own?"

"Since…forever," I tell her. "Why do you think I had no interest in going to college?"

Marty huffs a breath. "Did Mom know? She must've, right?"

"Yeah, she knew," I reply. "But when my teacher told her, she refused to believe it. I think it embarrassed her, that there was something wrong with me. I told Nate when we were married, and Mylo picked up on it immediately at the library. But other than that, I kept it to myself."

"I don't understand," Marty says. "How could Mom just refuse to do something about it? The school emails me whenever the kids don't turn in their homework. We're not even allowed to bake cookies for their classes unless the recipe is allergy-approved by the teacher."

"Things were different when we were kids," Jackie clarifies.

"Yeah," I agree. "Mom essentially told me to suck it up and try harder. I did what I could to pass my classes, and then left town right after graduation. I pursued a career where I didn't have to read."

"Jesus, Sammy," Marty says, his hand covering his gaping mouth. "So you can't read? Like, at all?"

Jackie barks out a laugh.

I roll my eyes. "Of course, I know *how* to read. It just takes me a lot longer than it does other people. I do it if I have to with contracts, bills, or other important documents, but aside from that, I try to avoid it."

They each give me a hug, and then pull me in for a final Rodriguez group hug, which lifts my spirits enough to clamber up the stairs and help them sort through Mom's clothes. It takes hours to empty out the closet and her dresser as we stop to reminisce the moment we recognize a shirt or dress. The task wipes me out, and once we're done, Marty and Jackie join me in the living room for a little mindless TV watching.

I drift off at one point, but the moment, "Baby gate!" "Dehydration!" and "Sepsis!" jolt me back awake, Jackie tucks my hair behind my ear and whispers, "Go back to sleep, Sam. It's okay. Marty and I are here."

That's all it takes to send me into the most restful sleep I've had in weeks.

CHAPTER 15

MYLO

Story hour with Uma Sinner is a smashing success. The kids bounce and cheer with each turn of the page, and she nurtures their excitement with an endless well of her own.

Though we have received some complaints via email from Sudbury residents who don't seem to understand what drag performers do, and there was that one incident of graffiti sprayed on our front windows. Overall, the townsfolk here seem extremely pleased, and that's all that matters to me.

After Councilman Grady denied my request to have security cameras installed around the exterior of the building, I paid to have them installed myself, so I don't anticipate any further property damage. None where we'll be unable to identify the source, anyway.

As Uma picks up another short book to read, I pull out the calendar to see how soon Uma is able to return, but activity in the parking lot catches my eye. Officer Burton, along with three other officers, burst through the front door.

"I'm sorry, folks, but we're shutting down this event," he says, addressing the parents whose mouths all hang open in shared confusion.

I step forward, trying to remain calm despite how uneasy I feel in his presence. "Officer Burton, I–"

"This isn't your call, Monroe," he replies, disdain thick in his tone when he says my last name. "We've gotten several calls at the station from concerned citizens, and I can't allow this atrocious display to continue any longer. Not in front of our kids."

I'm not following. "What display are you referring to?"

He gestures to Uma, who looks unsurprised, but I can see the hurt in her gaze as she closes the book she's holding and drops it in her lap.

It seems his problem with this event is similar to the emails we've received. It is such foolishness and a complete waste of energy to hate someone simply because of who they are. But there seems to be a significant level of vitriol for drag queens in general.

I refuse to accept it. "This is story hour, Officer Burton. We did not collect the children of Sudbury at their homes and force them to attend," I explain. "Their parents are here with them because they knew this would be a fun afternoon."

Out of the corner of my eye, I notice Charlie slowly receding into the crowd and heading to the back of the library as if trying to hide. I find it slightly odd, but again, I don't blame her. I make a note to myself to ask her about it later, though.

Officer Burton shrugs as he rests his hand on the pistol in his belt. "Don't care. The people of Sudbury know the world would be a better place without these kinds of people, and that's who I serve."

Wow, he's not even trying to hide his prejudice. "I see," I tell him, seething now. "So you serve only a handful of people in this town, and those people share the same disgusting, idiotic, and blatantly hateful views as you. Is that what you're telling us?"

He smirks as he unbuttons the strap that keeps the gun in his holster, then steps toward the table I've covered with my favorite romance novels. His beady eyes scan the covers and widen when he reaches for a book with two men on the cover. "See this?" he says, holding the book up for everyone. "I can tell just by looking at this book that it contains sexually explicit content, and it's right where any child can grab it."

I roll my eyes at his weak attempt to question the way I run the library. "The bottom of the sign says these books are best suited for those eighteen and older."

"This," he says, shaking the book, "is offensive and disrespects the traditional values held by the majority of Sudbury residents."

"The majority, really?" I question. If I were to ask for data on how many people in the town have a problem with a gay romance novel in the library, I would guess that no more than six people would protest its presence. This is utterly ridiculous.

He starts looking through the rest of the books on the table, pushing books aside as he goes. Several land on the floor, and I hear more than one tiny child gasp.

The other officers join in, knocking books off display tables and shelves in such a destructive manner that I will be amazed if none of the spines are dented by their search.

"We'll need to shut this place down until we can have every book in this facility evaluated by city council," Burton says with a sneer.

Anger rises like a tidal wave inside my gut. "You plan to go through every book in the building? That would take months."

"Maybe even longer," Burton says, smirking. "The council is far too busy with other, more pressing business to dedicate much time to this. And I'm sorry to inform you, but the library's needs are at the bottom of their list of priorities."

Oh, I am well aware of that, given I still have not even met Councilman Grady. He seems to have enough time on his hands to deny my requests, however. "You cannot do that."

My draxilio growls low enough that no one else can hear it, but it's enough to let me know how eager he is to be released and melt the skin off Burton's face.

"I can, actually," Burton says, tossing the gay romance novel back onto the messy pile of books that was a beautiful display only moments ago. Two of the younger officers stand on both sides of the front door, holding it open. "Time to go, folks," Burton says, waving them toward the door. "Thanks for your cooperation."

The parents, looking shocked and angry, ultimately follow Burton's command, picking up their kids and heading into the parking lot.

Uma grabs her things, and despite the situation, holds her head high as she goes to leave. Before she reaches the door, I stop her and quietly say, "I am so sorry this is happening. This will get sorted out and we can find another time for story hour, yes?"

She smiles, but there's sadness in her eyes. "It's not that simple. I need to go where I'm celebrated, not ostracized." Uma pats my arm, a clear goodbye. "Best of luck, Mylo."

I understand her dismissal. It hurts my heart to think she will never return to our humble library and the kids won't get to experience her delightful presence again, but she's right. It is not her responsibility to prove to Officer Burton or anyone else that she isn't the threat he makes her out to be. And though Burton singled her out, it's not why he's doing this. No, this is about me and the problem he continues to have with me and my brothers.

Shutting down story hour and closing the library to "evaluate each book for offensive or explicit content" is his way of destroying my reputation in the most public way possible. I wonder if there is a legal way for me to fight this. I'm sure he targeted the drag story hour specifically because there was nothing I could do to stop him. It wouldn't even surprise me to learn he was the one who graffitied our windows where Uma's posters were displayed. He seems intent on either putting us behind bars or driving us out of Sudbury.

But I refuse to run from this. If a fight is what Officer Burton wants, that's what he'll get.

As soon as the last car pulls out of the parking lot, I stride toward him. "You're not going to get away with this, you know. Shut down the library for a month, or even a year," I tell him, holding my arms out wide. "I'm not going anywhere, and when this crooked book evaluation is complete, I'll be right here, offering stacks of gay romance novels for the whole town to read."

"You need to lower your voice, son, or I'll be forced to charge you with disturbing the peace," he says, the grip on his pistol tightening.

"I...am not your son," I growl, unable to conceal my rage for another moment.

I can smell the fear that pools in his gut the closer I get to him. He is clearly threatened by my size, and I take a deep inhale, savoring the bitter scent. He has not even seen my winged form, and he's already this terrified? What a thrill it would be to wrap my claws around his thin, weak neck and snap it in half with a single squeeze.

He holds up a hand. "Take a step back, Monroe."

I don't move. I hold his gaze, letting the growl deep within my chest rise to the surface. Burton furrows his brow as he glares at me. Can he tell there's a murderous beast inside me, aching to be released?

"Get out of my library, or I will remove you myself," I grit, knowing it won't lead to anything good, but unable to stop the words from falling out of my mouth. He doesn't belong here surrounded by the brilliant words and stories that have shaped this world. In here lies knowledge and facts—both of which he seems averse to. He pulls his gun out of his holster, and I can't help but laugh at how long it took him to reach this point. The barrel of the gun is aimed at my chest, and I take a step closer, daring him to pull the trigger.

"Hands up!" the officer to his right shouts, and it doesn't take long for all four officers to have their guns trained on me. There's no danger to me even if they were to shoot me, but that's not something I want happening in the library.

I do as they say, raising my hands above my head while accepting that I must act as a human would in this moment. "Whoa, whoa, whoa," I say, stepping back.

"Freeze!" Burton shouts.

The other officers inch closer until they have me surrounded in a tight circle. Burton turns me around as he yanks my wrists behind my back. "Mylo Monroe, you're under arrest for threatening a police officer and disturbing the peace." He rattles off useless terms relating to the charges before reading me my rights, which occurs precisely the way I've seen on TV. This realization provides little comfort, considering how much trouble I appear to be in.

Officer Burton tugs me by my shackled hands out the front doors and into the parking lot. He pushes my head down as he shoves me into the back of the police car, my legs immediately cramping from the lack of room. Though I doubt a complaint about legroom would be welcomed at the moment.

Flashbacks of the day we broke Axil out of his jail cell flood my mind on the way there, and I wonder when I'll see him and the rest of my family again. Officer Burton leads me to the back of the station when we arrive, and he can barely contain his glee when my handcuffs are removed, and he locks me into my metal cage.

He flings the key ring around his middle finger, and as he turns the corner, I actually hear his laughter. He's *laughing* at me.

Is he so bored policing the quiet town of Sudbury that making an arrest excites him? What is wrong with this shell of a man?

Kill him, my draxilio urges. *Stomp on his throat while he sleeps.*

I cannot, I send back. I wish I could, because at this point, there is nothing that would delight me more than being the one to end Officer Burton's reign over this town. As a bonus, end his life too. But too much has happened. They would convict me immediately. It's not a death any of us could get away with. Not after he's made it clear how much he despises us.

Leaning against the cold cell bars, I ponder how to undo this predicament. Who do I speak to about ensuring the library stays open? Who would care? Is there a government body that polices the police? Can they be trusted to deliver justice?

My head begins to ache with the many possibilities of how this can only lead to my unemployment, and this town losing the only place for people to gather and discuss literature. I take a seat on the steel bench and lean my back against the bars of my cell, my mind drifting to Samantha. Visions of her smile, the feel of her soft tummy, and the scent of her perfume provide enough comfort to keep me from shifting inside this cell and burning this entire station to ash.

It takes hours, but eventually my request is granted to make a phone call. I call Axil and tell him to spread the word. His growl is steady and intimidating as he agrees, vowing to snuff the life out of

Officer Burton's eyes. I remind him not to say such things, at least not during this call, and he composes himself before hanging up.

My bail is posted by early evening, and Zev, Kyan, and Axil are waiting in the front lobby of the police station when I leave. "We are going to Tipsy's," Zev says, throwing an arm over my shoulder. "You look like you could use some cheering up."

Tipsy's is relatively quiet tonight with just a few men in the back of the bar playing pool and one at the end of the bar eating nuts and watching a sporting event on the big TV.

Vanessa wraps her small hands around my middle and squeezes tightly. "I was so worried about you. Are you okay?"

"I am…well enough," I reply. Truthfully, I'm not well at all, but rage fills me with enough adrenaline to fake it.

Izzy looks as if ready to draw blood.

Charlie is here, and the first thing I do is apologize.

"What? You have nothing to apologize for," she says, pulling out her phone. She shows me photos she took of the moment the cops arrived and everything that unfolded after. "I'm sending them to the local paper tonight."

Izzy hands me a mojito, and the moment the liquid touches my tongue, I realize how thirsty I am and swallow it in one gulp. They take the empty glass from my hand and refill it, and I continue to drink in an effort to numb the embarrassment.

"What will that accomplish?" I ask, pessimism clouding my thoughts.

"Public outrage is the best kind of pressure to put on crooked cops," she says, shaking her head. "I don't know if it'll fix the issues with the library, but it can't hurt."

"Then what?" Izzy asks. "You think this town's most respected police officer is going to get fired for spewing homophobia?"

Charlie purses her lips. "Not likely, but maybe he'll get suspended or assigned to a pile of paperwork that keeps him off our streets."

"Is that the best-case scenario here?" Kyan asks, his tone haughty. "What is the point of a law if it isn't even upheld by those in power?"

Izzy and Charlie exchange a glance before they both burst out laughing.

"Are you new here?" Charlie asks.

Kyan scoffs as he empties a bottle of light beer.

"What can be done to change this?" Zev asks, his gaze intense as it remains locked on Charlie.

"Well," Charlie says with a sigh, "we need a more powerful ally."

Zev scratches his chin. "What does that mean?" He looks at each of us, fear in his eyes. "If we cannot make a more powerful ally, we are at the mercy of Officer Burton. He'll do whatever he wants to us and likely get away with it."

"What are we supposed to do?" Kyan asks. "Leave town? Move again?"

"No," Axil replies immediately, wrapping Vanessa in a possessive embrace. "We have lived here for sixteen years. This is just as much our town as it is his."

"Who is above Officer Burton?" Izzy asks. "The mayor?"

Charlie pulls out her phone and starts typing. "Um, yeah, and the current mayor's term ends next year."

There it is. The solution to our problems is right in front of us. I can see it as clear as day. "It is settled," I say, getting to my feet. "I shall run for mayor of Sudbury."

CHAPTER 16

MYLO

"You are not running for mayor," Luka says, his arms crossed and his expression stony as he shakes his head. "Absolutely not."

He drove up for the night so that Harper and Ryan can do Vanessa's sonogram, and they brought their sons, Hudson and Cooper, with them. They have set up a makeshift medical suite in one of Vanessa's spare bedrooms, which is where the sonogram took place, and ultimately where she will deliver her and Axil's child. The sonogram went well, or as well as a sonogram of a half-alien fetus can go. Ryan was unable to tell the sex of the child, but the heartbeat was strong and the fetus appeared healthy.

Vanessa has been staring dreamily at the sonogram photo for the last hour and isn't paying any attention to our conversation. I don't blame her. Axil informed Luka of my plans as soon as the sonogram was complete, and as predicted, Luka does not approve.

"Do you have any idea how quickly that level of exposure could destroy us?" he asks.

Harper and Ryan are busy putting their medical tools away while the boys snack on the chips and salsa Vanessa set out for them.

I understand where Luka is coming from, but we are out of options.

"In order to fight Burton, we need power. Right now, we have none. Having one of us in a political role gives us power, and clearly, I am the best candidate for the job."

"I don't agree," Kyan says. "I look much more presidential than you do."

Luka huffs a breath, already out of patience. "No one is running for president, and no one is running for mayor."

"Mom, can I be president one day?" Cooper asks, his brown eyes an exact copy of Harper's in their size and color.

"No!" Luka shouts. "No, you cannot."

"But he was born here," Hudson points out, his horns starting to curl back at the top. "That's all it takes, right?"

He has grown so much since the last time I saw him. They both have. I remember when Hudson was born, Luka's biggest fear was that he'd be unable to mask. He feared he would need to keep his boy hidden from the world.

But the practice started immediately, even with just Luka masking in front of Baby Hudson, so he could see how it was done. By age two, Hudson was masking on his own, and Cooper picked it up before he uttered his first word.

Their natural skin color is a pale blue, no doubt due to their human genes, and though it took them longer to shift than the average draxilio, and their beasts are smaller than ours, their fires are strong, and their fangs are terrifyingly sharp. They are brilliant, thoughtful boys, and being in their presence fills me with overwhelming joy.

"That's not all it takes," Harper clarifies, "But yes, it's a requirement."

"What are you doing?" Luka asks Harper. "Do not encourage these thoughts."

She shrugs. "Maybe by the time Coop is old enough to run for president, we've figured out a way to keep this big secret hidden. Anything is possible."

"No," Luka argues. "This is not possible." He looks at Cooper. "You running for president is not possible." Then his eyes find mine. "You running for mayor is not possible."

"Luka," Axil begins in an attempt to calm him, but Luka cuts him off.

"Do not start," he replies, holding up a hand. "I know you wish to ease my fears, but you cannot." He looks around the room, taking a moment to focus on each of us. "Do you understand what we have here? Look at what we have built. You wish to put our happiness at risk to sate your need for vengeance?"

It is Luka who doesn't seem to understand. "All I am trying to do is ensure our safety," I tell him.

Cooper lets out a dramatic sigh. "Ugh, can we have tacos now?"

"Yeah," Hudson agrees. "This is boring, and we're hungry."

Ryan bursts out laughing. "I know this is an important discussion, but I'm with them."

Harper puts her medical bag away, grabs her cane, and pulls her sons in for a hug, then pinches the tips of their noses. "Got 'em. And I'm keeping them."

"Mom, we know you didn't actually steal our noses," Hudson mutters with an eye roll.

Cooper agrees. "We're too old for that game."

Harper gasps in mock surprise. "Um, you're never too old for that game, understand?" She strides across the room, and tucks herself under Luka's arm, then leans up on her toes to plant a kiss on his cheek. "Let's put a pin in this for now. Your overbearing, big brother schtick can resume once our bellies are full. Sound good, my love?"

It pains him to relent, but even I can see the slight pull of his lips into a grin as he gazes down at his mate. He nods with a cranky huff, and we make our way into Vanessa's tiny kitchen as we fill our plates with tacos.

"Doc, don't forget to tell Vanessa about the…" Ryan says, his voice lowering and his eyebrows lifting as he trails off. "The…you know."

Vanessa, mid-bite, drops her taco onto the plate and waits with a nervous gaze. "Hmm?"

Harper sighs as she gives Ryan a stern look. "I thought we weren't going to share it until we had more data?"

Ryan chuckles. "Oh come on. It's exciting! Plus, you have to show them your new party trick."

Putting her plate on the counter, Harper finishes chewing, wipes her mouth, and strides into the living room, opening one of the large windows overlooking the cornfield across the river. "Ryan and I have been studying my DNA since Luka and I became mates, and we've noticed that my cells have changed significantly over the last sixteen years."

Vanessa clears her throat and reaches for Axil's hand. "What does that mean?"

Harper chews nervously on the inside of her cheek. "Well, I'm not...entirely human anymore."

"What!" Axil shouts, getting to his feet.

Vanessa stands and places a hand on his chest. Immediately, the tension fades from his shoulders. "Harper, I'm going to need you to say more right now."

"I'm not saying I'm turning into a draxilio, but my body can do things it couldn't before. Things that are distinctly draxilio traits."

"Such as?" Vanessa prods.

Harper purses her lips, "Just watch." She sticks her head out the window and takes a deep inhale. The rest of us jump up from our chairs and crowd around her at the window as she exhales, sending a miniature ball of fire into the air.

Vanessa gasps, her mouth hanging open as she tries to process what we all just saw.

Ryan claps excitedly. "Isn't that cool?"

"Y-you can breathe fire?" Axil asks, confused, but still anxious about what this means for Vanessa.

"Does that mean I can breathe fire?" Vanessa asks, walking to the window.

Harper steps out of her way. "I don't know. It took years for me to gain that ability, but everyone's different. Give it a shot."

Vanessa breathes in deeply, then lets out a surprisingly loud burp on her exhale. "Oh jesus. Excuse me."

The boys cackle at Vanessa's belch, and Luka hushes them with a stern expression on his face.

Harper closes the window and takes Vanessa by both hands, leading her back to her seat in the kitchen. "Don't worry. Whatever changes are meant to happen to you, they'll come with time. And just so you know, I can't shift. I can't fly, and nothing else about me is different. That's it. That's the only thing."

"Well," Ryan interjects. "It's not the only thing. We think the aging process has slowed way down as well."

"Really?" I ask, hope surging through my chest. With the pitifully short life span of humans, my brothers and I have been concerned what that would mean once we found mates. Would we be forced to live another five hundred years without them once they passed away? Would our life spans be shortened once we got here?

"Yeah," Ryan replies. "Luka's DNA hasn't changed, so it seems like he'll reach the typical seven-hundred-year mark, and now I think Harper might age at the same rate."

Axil says nothing as he strides directly toward Luka and pulls him in for a tight embrace. "I am thrilled for you, brother. For us."

Luka returns the hug and ends it with an awkward pat on Axil's back. "Yes, it is a massive relief. I have no interest in existing without Harper, and now, hopefully, I will not have to."

Vanessa cries as Axil pulls her into his arms. The rest of us remain quiet as we watch the two of them hold each other, and I'm certain Zev and Kyan are as lost in thought as I am, thrilled that a long future with our mates now seems possible, while still curious about how this genetic shift will present in Vanessa and the other human females who join our family. Will they all be able to breathe fire? Or will they gain different abilities?

Eventually, Cooper and Hudson squabble about whose flame is bigger out of the two of them, and it lightens the mood enough for us to return to our food.

I can't help but think of Lady Norton, Vanessa's late aunt, as we enjoy our feast in the home that was once hers. The sight of her niece sitting on Axil's lap, pregnant with his child, the half-human, half-draxilio children laughing and throwing tortilla chips at one another across the table, and me and my brothers together, maybe not united as one, but still a unit. An unshakable alien family doing everything they can to keep one another safe.

The only thing missing from this heartwarming scene is Samantha.

CHAPTER 17

SAM

*M*arty, Jackie, and I are making progress with the house, and at their urging—demand, rather—I've started showering regularly again. I'm not sure I'll ever feel like I've caught up on sleep, but with each night I don't wake up screaming and crying, I inch closer to being fully rested. While my days are occupied with sorting through Mom's belongings, my nights are quieter than I'd like them to be.

Vanessa and I FaceTime every night before bed, but I can't bring myself to go visit her. Seeing Axil will remind me of Mylo, and that'll send me backsliding into a pit of depression. I need to be gentle with myself right now, and that means keeping my distance.

But having no one to cuddle with or plans to keep me busy, I find myself lying in bed flipping through old photo albums to see Mom again, or scrolling through my old photos on Instagram and wishing I could hop on a plane and relive these moments over and over. Watching the aurora borealis from my private igloo in Finland, bird watching in Chile, eating fried silkworms in Thailand, and so many more.

Suddenly, I find myself looking up flights and hotel rates, and trying to decide where to run off to next. For a split second, my heart sinks at the realization that I can't leave, that I need to stay here. But then I remember there's nothing keeping me in Sudbury. If I want to jet off somewhere, I can.

But where? Ireland, maybe? I haven't been to the Emerald Isle in years, and I love how it never gets too hot there. Although, it's been even longer since I've attended a Tuscan wine tasting. Tuscany is so beautiful, and the smaller cities scattered throughout the region are some of my favorite places to explore. I haven't been to Siena yet, and I've heard nothing but good things.

My thoughts immediately turn to Mylo, and the poems he read to me in Italian. I bet he would love Tuscany.

No, I chide myself. Mylo is not mine. If I'm planning a trip, it's going to be a solo adventure. That's how I've always traveled. I used to get so much pride out of my ability to see the world on my own, but as I scroll through flights to Florence, there's a hollowness in my gut that won't fade.

Ignoring it, I pull out my suitcase and start tossing my clothes inside. I don't need to fold anything as long as I take my mini steamer. Digging that out of my dresser, I toss that in too. Before I throw in my bras and panties, my phone vibrates, and Vanessa's face pops up on my screen.

"Hey," I greet her as I open FaceTime. "I'm a little busy at the moment, Vanilla. Can I call you back in a litt–"

"Emergency!" she shouts.

"What?" I ask, dropping everything in my hands except the phone. "What's wrong? Is it the baby? Are you going into labor?"

"No, no, nothing like that," she says with a smile.

A deep breath whooshes out of me. "Thank god. Then what?"

"It's a friend emergency. I need you to come to my place right away."

"Why? What's going on?"

She shakes her head. "I'll explain when you get here. Just come now. Okay? Bye."

I don't stop to check my hair or clothes before shoving my feet into my ratty Sambas and grabbing my keys as I race out the door. Whatever is going on with Vanessa is too important to fret over vanity. Plus, she won't care that my hair is dirty and my sweatpants have a spaghetti stain just above the knee.

My journey begins with a run-walk that starts to feel foolish after a few feet, so I break into a jog, and find that the burn of my muscles feels surprisingly good. It's been far too long since I moved my body, and that just makes me run harder.

When I arrive, Vanessa throws open the door and greets me with arms wide open. "Samwich! You made it."

"Yeah," I mutter through panting breaths. "I ran here." She leads me inside, and in her living room, I find Zev, Kyan, Axil, and, of course, Mylo. And here I am, looking like a sweaty beast.

There's no backing out of this now. Which was obviously Vanessa's plan all along as she locks the front door and shoots me a wink.

"So there was no emergency?" I ask, not pissed at her deception, but definitely annoyed.

"No, that was true," she says, patting the empty chair next to Zev. "Mylo's planning on running for mayor, and we need you to tell him what a horrible idea it is."

"That's it?" I ask before locking eyes with Mylo. The sight of him still makes my heart race, and part of me is glad that hasn't gone away. "That plan sucks. Don't run for mayor."

Mylo throws up his hands. "You too? Really?"

Kyan snickers. "It's unanimous. You cannot run for mayor now. Someone call Luka. He will be thrilled to hear Mylo was finally forced to abandon this foolish pursuit."

"How else are we supposed to protect our family from Officer Burton?" Mylo asks.

They fill me in on the bullshit that occurred during Uma Sinner's story hour, and I'm disgusted, but not surprised that Officer Burton would stoop so low.

"Charlie is planning on sending pictures she took to the local paper," Mylo explains, "but I'm not convinced Officer Burton will be held accountable." He looks defeated, and it sends a fresh surge of vengeance through my blood. If there wasn't a one hundred percent chance of me going straight to jail, I'd punch Officer Burton in the teeth.

That would probably hurt my hand, though. Hmm. The nose. Yeah, that's better, and much easier to break.

Vanessa hands me a bowl of popcorn, and I notice everyone else has their own bowl as well. What a cozy little trap she set for me. Sneaky minx.

"Mylo," I begin, tossing a piece into my mouth. "The moment you announce you're running for office, it doesn't matter how high or low that position is, your personal life gets ripped apart and dissected, and this all happens publicly."

"That's precisely what Charlie said," Zev exclaims proudly, shaking his head in awe.

"And what Luka said," Axil points out.

I'm not sure what that expression on Zev's face is all about, but it doesn't seem important at the moment, so I continue. "Do you really want people poking around in your past, digging up secrets that could put you and your family in danger?"

Mylo sighs. "That would not be ideal."

"No," Axil agrees. "It certainly would not."

Pushing his glasses up the bridge of his nose, he stares into space for a few moments as he thinks about this. His gray eyes eventually drift back to mine. "Ah, you are right. It's too risky."

Vanessa leans on the back of Mylo's chair and pats him on the arm. "Told you. Sorry, bro."

Zev groans. "Charlie said those exact words days ago. Why did it take hearing them from Sam's mouth to convince you?"

Mylo's gaze drops to my lips, and they don't seem to move away. This goes on for several seconds until Vanessa elbows Mylo in the arm. "Huh?" He looks up at Vanessa. "Did you say something?"

Laughter fills the room at Mylo's inability to focus, but I don't find it funny at all. It just makes me want him more than I did, which was already quite a lot. I miss talking to him. I miss the way he held me after sex, and the softness in his voice when he'd read to me. I miss everything about him.

After a few more rounds of Mylo's brothers telling him he cannot run for mayor, Zev and Kyan bid us farewell. Zev is eager to resume practicing with his new guitar, and Kyan grumbles about having to go into the office early the next day.

I hug Vanessa before I go, thanking her for giving me a reason to leave the house, and she pulls me into a corner of the dining room. "I have the photos Charlie took of what happened at the library," she whispers. "She was going to send them to the paper, but I thought it might make more of an impact coming from you."

"Me?"

"Yeah, with your resume and portfolio, they're more likely to take it seriously. I'll text you the photos as soon as you leave. Send them to the Concord Chronicle, okay? And, you never know. It could lead to other things. Paid assignments, even."

I nod, appreciating her support. "I'll reach out to them tonight."

Vanessa hugs me again at the front door, and Mylo follows me to the edge of her driveway.

"How've you been?" I ask, then immediately regret the question. "I mean, other than your arrest."

He shoves his hands into his pockets and rocks back and forth on his heels, making him look like a shy teenager rather than the centuries-old dragon shifter he is. "Other than that humiliating hiccup, uh, I have been well, yes. The kids loved drag story hour, and I think the parents did too."

"I'm so sorry Officer Burton ruined it," I tell him, desperate to reach for him. To provide even a sliver of solace to his otherwise trash heap of a day.

He scrubs a hand down his face. "That little man seems intent on destroying us. There has to be some way to stop him."

I know he's not expecting an answer, but I still wish I could give him one.

"Well, I should head home," I say, swatting away the mosquitos that are suddenly flying around my head. I want Mylo to invite me over to his place. Or offer to walk me home. Anything. Even five more minutes in his company would be nice.

"Actually, can you wait here? I have something for you."

"Yes. Yes, I'll wait." I don't care how eager or desperate I sound. Mylo has a gift for me. I stare at his perfectly sculpted ass as he jogs toward his house, and I have to fan myself as soon as he disappears inside.

He returns with a wrapped gift the size of a manila envelope, and I tear into it the second he hands it over.

"Oh my god," I gasp as I stare at the framed photo of Mom and me asleep in her bed, our heads nestled together and our fingers entwined between us. He must've taken it while he was reading to her. The soft light from the lamp on her nightstand cascades over the side of her face, making her look ten years younger and so peaceful. "You took this?"

He nods, the dimple in his cheek accentuated by the moonlight. "The second time I came over to read to your mom. Do you remember? She put her head on your shoulder and quickly fell asleep. Then, about five minutes later, you leaned into her and fell asleep too."

"Yeah, I remember," I choke out, my eyes filling with tears. The memory is fresh in my mind. His voice is just so soothing that I passed out instantly. Or maybe it's not his voice, specifically, but his presence. When he's near, I feel safe. "Thank you so much." I launch myself at him, and he catches me easily, holding my body against his. Slowly, I draw back, and I don't know if I make the first move, or he does, but suddenly his lips are on mine.

Maybe I haven't ruined this. Maybe there's a chance for us after all.

A second later, my hopes are dashed as he pulls away, holding me at a distance by my shoulders much like he did in the mop closet at Mom's funeral. "I'm sorry, Samantha. I'm sorry for everything I said at the hospital. I regret my words. But I'm also sorry because we can't do this."

"But wouldn't it be a lot of fun if we did?" I ask, half-serious, half-teasing.

He shakes his head solemnly. "I care about you. Deeply," he says, releasing me. "I want you to be happy, but I also want me to be happy, and unless you're ready for something real, then I must remain your friend and nothing more."

Am I ready for something real? I'm no longer a caregiver, so that's not a reason to hesitate. However, if I go back to working the way I was before, any relationship we started would be mostly long distance. Even if I requested more assignments close to home, my job keeps me on the road a lot. Would Mylo be interested in a long-distance relationship?

Then there's the issue of his draxilio, and this whole red-eye situation. I don't know much about the way the mate bond is formed among his species, but when Axil's eyes turned red, it was in front of Vanessa, and it was the moment his draxilio and his flightless form became aligned on the idea of her being the one. It was a silent agreement, of sorts, between the two parts of Axil's soul that Vanessa was their perfect match.

I know Mylo's draxilio adores me, and if he wants a relationship with me, why haven't his eyes turned red? Shouldn't that mean that they're aligned? That I'm the one for them? Or am I setting myself up for heartbreak? What if I tell Mylo I'm ready for something real tonight and tomorrow his eyes turn red for someone else?

That would crush me. And I wouldn't just be losing Mylo, I'd be losing Vanessa in a way too. Sure, we'd stay friends, but the distance would grow between us the moment Mylo's eyes turned red. His mate would become part of the group, and I don't know if I could handle watching another woman hang all over him.

There are too many unknowns to make him a promise I can't keep, so I offer only what I can. "Friends it is," I say, holding out my hand.

His hand dwarfs mine as he shakes it. "Friends."

CHAPTER 18

MYLO

*M*y draxilio continues to berate me in my dreams that night, and the entire next day. *You colossal fool. She was right there. She wanted you and you pushed her away.*

Yes, I am agreeing with you, I send back. I hate myself for causing the hurt in her big brown eyes, but she doesn't seem to know what she wants, and I cannot return to being her sex friend when my heart wants more. *I assure you I did this to protect both of us.*

I weigh eight tons and can spit fire. Your protection is not something I require. Stop being an idiot and go devour our mate's hot cunt.

Not our mate, I point out.

Part of me wants to blame him for my eyes not turning red for Samantha. But that would be like blaming two buns for not being a cheeseburger. There is a fundamental element to this equation that's still missing, and it's not his fault it hasn't happened.

"You okay?" Izzy asks, sliding a second mojito in my direction.

I shrug. "I'm fine. City council has decided to put me on leave while they conduct their book evaluation, and I can't set foot in the library until they decide my fate."

Izzy leans both elbows on the bar, eyes rolling. "Such bullshit. Did Charlie hear back from the newspaper?"

"I have not heard anything," I explain.

"Hmm. I'm sure she'll reach out as soon as they respond." Izzy grabs a rag from a lower shelf and begins wiping the bar clean.

The next person that enters the bar is Samantha, and though my life feels as if it's unraveling, the sight of her calms me a bit. "Hey," I say with a smile. "What are you doing here?"

"I'm here for you," she says as if it should be obvious. She orders a Moscow mule as she pulls her phone from her purse and scrolls through her email. "I sent Charlie's photos to the paper last night, and I spent most of the morning at their offices."

"Really?" I ask, hope surging in my chest. "What did they say?"

"Well, they're definitely going to cover it," she replies. "The editor I spoke with was appalled by what went down at the library, especially since kids were present. He also didn't seem surprised to hear that Burton was leading the book ban and went on to show me several clips of stories he's written over the years covering Burton's shady behavior."

I am speechless. It seemed pointless to pursue this given how much power Burton has, but it comforts me to know that people actually care about the library being shut down and the nonsensical reason why. "You think this will lead to…something?"

She sighs heavily as she stares at the drink in front of her. "I honestly don't know," then the corners of her lips form a sneaky grin, "but now that I'm officially employed as one of the Concord Chronicle's photographers, I plan on exposing Officer Burton the first chance I get."

"What? They hired you?" Did Samantha willingly take a job that will keep her here? I never would have expected that.

She is quick to wave a dismissive hand. "Well, it's a freelance gig, and the assignments I get will probably be sporadic, but I'm optimistic. I was thinking I could pitch a story on the *Bridgerton* event, using the photos I took, and maybe interview some of the kids from story hour and their parents on how the library has improved their lives. This connection with the paper can only help us, right?"

I know she speaks of our group, and not just her and me, but when she utters the word "us," my stomach flips.

"I'm not going to let him ruin your reputation, Mylo," she adds, her tone serious.

"Thank you," I say, moved by her dedication to help me out of this. I open my mouth to ask if she'd like to leave Tipsy's and come back to my house, but Charlie strolls in and the moment is lost.

Samantha greets Charlie with a hug, thanking her for taking the photos, and repeats what she told me about the newspaper covering the story. Charlie seems invigorated by the update, and I notice her fist clenching at her side. "We'll get him. This town deserves better than the oppressive rule of a crooked cop."

That gives me an idea. "Charlie, have you considered running for local office?"

The giggle that escapes her lips is small, quiet, and controlled, but it escalates quickly into a loud, wild cackle as she slaps her hand on the bar. "Definitely not," she says. "I have kind of a sordid past with the world of politics." She takes a sip of her drink. "Don't get me wrong, I could win. I was the chief of staff for a mayor for a spell, so I know how to navigate that life."

"Were you, really?" I don't recall seeing that on her resume.

Samantha nods. "That's incredible."

"It's not the way I want to live, though," she adds. "This is a fresh start for me, and now I'm all about quiet and privacy."

"Fair enough." I drain the rest of my drink and run a hand through my hair. "It's such a shame I can't run. I would be able to fund my entire campaign myself."

Charlie blinks several times as she stares at me. "I'm not sure if what I'm about to say crosses a line, and honestly, I mean no disrespect."

I'm certain what she's about to say won't offend me. "Right now, I'm not your boss since I'm on leave. So please, speak freely."

She smiles as she sits on the stool to my left and straightens her spine, summoning the courage. "Just because you're white and rich doesn't mean you should run for office."

"But how am I expected to make meaningful changes in this town?"

"Easy," she says. "Throw your money at the people in the community who are already doing the work, who genuinely care about making Sudbury better, and who would kill for a chance to be elected to local office."

"Okay, like who?"

She takes a moment to consider her answer. "Teachers, government employees, volunteers—there are plenty of people you could support if they ran."

Something from her resume pops into my head. "Aren't you a teacher?"

"I'm a part-time music teacher at the elementary school, and I teach beginner guitar to adults one night a week," she explains. "That's not what I meant."

"What did you mean, then?"

"I'll look deeper into potential candidates within the community," she explains. "There are usually groups who vet potential candidates, even for small, local roles, so part of the process might already be done."

"Whoever you deem best suited for the job, I shall fund their campaign."

Her eyes widen when they glance down at her phone. "Shit, I need to get home. I promised my daughter I'd make homemade mac and cheese with her."

That certainly gets my attention. "You have a daughter?"

"Yes, her name's Nia," she says casually. "Have I not mentioned her?"

"Aww, I love that name," Samantha adds.

"No, I'm certain I would have remembered the fact that you created a tiny version of yourself that lives in your house."

"Wow, you chose the most complicated way to describe having a child," Charlie says. "I'm impressed."

I offer her a mock-salute, and she laughs as she leaves.

More people filter into Tipsy's the later into the afternoon it gets, and at some point, Samantha says she has to meet her siblings back at her house. Our goodbye is awkward, and the heat between us remains. I decide to stay a bit longer if only to give my painfully obvious erection time to go down.

Every stool at the bar is full by the time I finish my fourth mojito and I hear the grating voice of Councilman Grady as he requests a beer. I recognize the tone from the few clips I watched when he won his position on the council. Unfortunately, we have never met in person. He takes a seat at the other end of the bar, but with my heightened senses, I can hear every word he says to the man next to him.

They get into a conversation about how drag shows don't fit with this town and that the people of Sudbury want a place where they can sit and have a beer without worrying if a man in a dress is about to hit on them. And "Jesus knows what they get up to in the restroom."

Izzy and I exchange a look of emotional exhaustion tinged with fear. It seems Officer Burton's reign isn't the only one we need to be worried about.

CHAPTER 19

SAM

*I*t took a week for the library to reopen, and two more for Mylo to be reinstated as head librarian, and that's only because of the story the Chronicle published on Mylo's arrest followed by the adorable slideshow of handmade cards that the story-hour kids mailed to the library, telling Mylo how much they missed him and how eager they were to see the library back up and running. City council folded like a cheap table when some of the story-hour parents showed up to their public forum demanding that Mylo get his job back.

Not even that was enough to press pause on my quest to bring Officer Burton down. I convinced my editor at the Chronicle to set up an anonymous tip line for anyone who wants to share abuses of power they've witnessed by the Sudbury police force, and almost all the tips we received were about Officer Burton. Cross-referencing the tips with public arrest records, the Chronicle published an opinion piece written by my editor, questioning if it's time to retire Burton's reputation as a highly respected officer, and hold him accountable for the monstrous acts he's committed over the years.

Several books were taken out of the library to be evaluated by city council, and we have no idea how long it'll take to get them back.

But victory came this morning when my editor texted me saying he'd heard that Officer Burton had been temporarily suspended with pay while an investigation into his past behavior is taking place. The fact that he is suspended with pay makes me want to crack skulls because he was essentially given a vacation for being a homophobic prick.

"It's not nothing," Charlie reminds me as I refill my cart with books that need to be put away. "It's the first punch in a long fight that we might not live to see the end of. But that first punch is everything. We just need to keep swinging."

I've gotten to know her quite a bit during Mylo's leave, and she's become one of my favorite people. She's tenacious and brilliant and one hell of a musician. With Mylo gone, I figured she might need some help, so I volunteered to run the returns cart around the library, shelving books.

Helping out at the library and working for the newspaper has made me realize that I'm not ready to get back on the road. Traveling for work and traveling for pleasure are two very different things, and though I know my wanderlust will never go away, I also don't think I want to spend the rest of my life living out of a suitcase. Putting down roots in one place won't prevent me from traveling wherever and whenever I want. I can still do that, but I'll also have a place to come home to.

I doubt I would've realized that without coming home to care for Mom.

Waking up early the following day, I go for a run around the neighborhood, shower, and throw on a pair of black tailored, wide-leg trousers, my platform Keds, and a blue crop top that matches the natural color of Mylo's skin. I throw my curls into a high ponytail and grab my camera as I head out the door.

There's a crowd of kiddos running around the library when I arrive, many clamoring for their chance to give Mr. Mylo a hug to celebrate his return. He hands out books to each child, and they race off to their designated spot to start reading. Today is the library's quarterly Read-A-Thon where kids ages three to ten can check out an unlimited number of books as long as they read them at the library.

Free snacks and beverages are provided throughout the day, and any child who reads five books or more by the time the library closes gets a gift certificate to Supreme Buns for three free sandwiches. The youngest participants are allowed to get help from a parent or guardian in an effort to foster a love of reading as early as possible.

At one point, I notice his nostrils flaring, and his eyes find me immediately. "Samantha," he says, his hand covering his heart. "You are here." His gaze drops to the camera hanging around my neck. "You brought your camera?"

"Yeah, I told Charlie I'd help pass out drinks and snacks, but between snack breaks, I'd walk around and take candid photos of the kids and send them to their parents."

He looks confused. "Did she offer to pay you for this?"

"No," I say with a chuckle. "I offered to do it for free."

"Why?"

"Well, don't go thinking I'm some selfless angel. I thought it would be a good opportunity to meet people and pass out my new business cards." I hand him one, and I watch as he glides his thumb over the glossy gold letters of my name.

"Sammy Rod Photography," he says, a smile playing on his perfect lips. "Wonderful. Well, thank you for doing this."

He seems stunned, and slightly skeptical of my presence here, but that's okay. I'd feel the same way if I were him. I'll tell him the rest of my plan later when he's not so busy.

Photographing children is surprisingly difficult, I quickly learn. Most of them don't seem to understand what candid means, and the moment I get close, they start hamming it up, smiling so wide I can count all the teeth they've lost. Then they want to tell me about each tooth, and the gifts the tooth fairy left under their pillow for said tooth.

The parents love the photos, and once I get at least one photo of each child, I ask the parents if there's a particular pose they'd like to see, or if they'd like to join their kids for an impromptu family photo.

I go from "Camera Lady," to "Juice Lady," to "Cracker Lady" in the span of an hour but having a group of kids cheering every time you walk by is an unexpected ego boost, and I eat up every bit of it.

Watching Mylo interact with the kids is the real treat, though. He's a natural with them, praising them when they finish a book and genuinely engaging with them on what they liked or didn't like. They adore him, which sends my heart into a constant flutter. It's not like I want kids of my own, but seeing this gentler, sillier side of him makes me love him even more.

Wait.

I...love him?

As soon as the realization hits, it seems ridiculous that I didn't come to it sooner. Of course, I love him. He's been a bright spot in my otherwise gloomy existence for the last few months. He read to me and actually made me fall in love with the concept of love. I feel it fully now, and only for him.

By the end of the day, Mylo hands out seventeen gift certificates to Supreme Buns, which is apparently a new record. The number of participants is growing each quarter, and the overwhelming joy on Mylo's face makes me melt. I help him and Charlie clean up, and when Mylo sets the alarm and locks up, I practically collapse in the parking lot from exhaustion.

"Man, kids are...a lot," I mutter, tightening my ponytail. "They're adorable and fearless, but also a lot."

Charlie laughs. "I detect no lies."

I say goodnight to Charlie and Mylo and start heading down the sidewalk toward my house, but a few minutes later, Mylo is yelling for me to wait up.

"Thank you again for your help today," he says, rubbing the back of his neck in a way that makes him look shy.

Mylo isn't shy. What's happening here?

"I wanted to ask. What will you do with those business cards?"

"Um, probably hand them to people?"

He laughs, and the throaty sound of it sends goose bumps across my skin. "I mean, will you be resuming your frequent work travel and shooting in Sudbury between your assignments?"

Finally, I get to tell him about my plans. "Oh, that. No, I'm not planning to go back on the road. Not for a while anyway, and it definitely won't be as often."

"Oh?"

"Yeah, I'd like to stick around. See what it's like to be a Sudburian as an adult, you know?" I furrow my brow teasingly.

His arm brushes against mine, and I realize he's walking closer to me. "So, you plan to stay."

"Yup," I tell him when we reach the end of my driveway. Then I turn to face him, letting my hand hover just above his arm. "I don't know, it just feels like the right time for something…real."

Before he can respond, I turn on my heel and hurry toward the front door. "Goodnight, Mylo," I call over my shoulder.

He chuckles, amused by my flirting. "Goodnight, Samantha."

The moment I'm inside, I wonder if I've made a mistake. Should I have waited to see his reaction? He said he only wanted me if I was ready for something real, and tonight I flat-out told him that something real is what I'm looking for. Then I ran inside.

What the hell is wrong with me?

Although maybe it was the right move. I'm as terrified of rejection as he is of getting his heart broken, so this way, he can go home and take some time to think about it instead of hastily agreeing just because I said what he wanted to hear. I also want to be sure he still wants to be with me.

At this point, I'm all in. I don't care that his eyes haven't turned red. I want to go to sleep to the sound of his voice as he reads to me, and I want to wake up in the safety of his arms.

The question is, does he feel the same way?

CHAPTER 20

SAM

*T*he sun wakes me by blasting me in the face through the window, and I smack my palm against my forehead for forgetting to close the blinds the night before. But once I'm up, I'm up, and it's a nice enough summer day so I open all the windows, throw on a sports bra and booty shorts, put my headphones on, and blast Busta Rhymes as I clean the floors.

When a song I don't recognize pops up, I reach for my phone to press skip, and I discover a text from Mylo.

Mylo: *Are you home? I need to speak with you. It's urgent.*

Hmm. What could this be about?

Me: *Yeah, I'm home. Is everything okay?*

My mind drifts to Vanessa.

Me: *Is it the baby?*

Mylo: *No, all is well with Vanessa. May I come now?*

Nerves tighten my stomach as I ponder a million possibilities. The one that sticks is the worst one of all. Perhaps he considered my plan to stay in town, and he realized that since the thrill of our secret hookups is gone, there's no point in making it official.

Or it could be that he's changed his mind about wanting a relationship and would prefer to go back to the anonymous sex that brought us together in the first place.

Or maybe his eyes have turned red for someone else since I last saw him and he's coming over to break the news.

Oh yeah, that last one is what I'm dreading the most.

I throw on a pair of sweats over my booty shorts before I let him in. His posture is stiff as he steps inside wearing sunglasses that he's never worn, and my palms start to sweat.

"You still cannot go up the stairs?" he asks.

"I can," I tell him. "I just hate looking at them," I shrug as I walk into the kitchen and pull a glass from the cupboard. "Not sure what to do about that long-term, but for now, I try not to think about...you know, what happened on them." I open the fridge, stalling. "Want some water? Or lemonade?"

"No, thank you," he replies. Ever the gentleman.

He still hasn't removed his sunglasses, and my heart sinks. Might as well get this over with.

"What did you want to talk about?"

He sighs heavily and slowly removes his sunglasses to reveal blood-red eyes. I was expecting his irises to be red, but that's not the case. His irises are the same gray shade that makes his beauty unique, but not so striking that he looks alien. The rest of his eyes, though, are definitely alien. The normally white part is what's bright red, and it's deeply unsettling to look at. He looks like he's on the verge of death. How did Vanessa not scream at the top of her lungs when Axil's eyes turned?

"Well?" he asks when I don't say anything.

But I'm not sure what he wants me to say. Congrats on finally finding your mate? Hope you two are very happy together? Hope she doesn't step on a landmine and get blown to pieces?

"Your eyes are red," I finally mutter. Then, in a quiet voice, "H-happy for you."

"You're happy for *me?*"

He sounds mad. Why would he be mad about this?

"Of course, I am," I tell him, forcing my lips into a smile that I hope looks genuine. "So, who's the lucky lady?"

Mylo tilts his head to the side, looking at me strangely. He takes a step forward. "Samantha, it's you."

"Me?"

"Yes."

I wasn't expecting that, and I still don't understand why he seems so pissed about it.

"I thought your eyes turned in front of your mate."

"Well, if you hadn't run inside so quickly last night, they would have." He rubs his eyes, and I remember hearing about how much they itch right before the color turns. "I almost clawed my eyes out on the way home," he says, confirming the itch. He sits on the couch and drops his head in his hands. "I didn't know what to do. I couldn't sleep at all. There's still part of me that wonders how we're supposed to proceed."

"What do you mean?" I ask. Isn't this a done deal? His eyes turned red for me, so I'm his mate. Seems simple enough, and I'm certainly not bothered by the outcome. Being with Mylo is what I want.

It's clearly not what he wants, though, based on the tortured expression he's wearing.

Frustration starts to grow the longer I look at his scowl. Would it really be so terrible to have me as a mate?

"I'm sorry this is such a bummer for you," I tell him, striding into the kitchen in a huff and pouring myself a glass of lemonade.

"Why would you say that?" he asks.

Seriously? "Look at you," I shout. "You're fucking miserable that I'm your mate."

He rises to his feet, his fists clenched at his sides as he yells, "I'm not miserable that you're my mate. I'm afraid that you will run."

"What?"

Is that truly the source of his anguish? He's worried I'm going to bolt at the first sign of trouble? I suppose it's not an unheard-of theory. Historically, that has been my move but only because there wasn't much for me to come home to.

Mylo's feet remain planted across the room. His chest heaves, and I can't tell if he's about to snap from rage or arousal, or both.

I'd prefer both.

"Samantha," he begins, his voice ragged. "I have loved you since the night we met, and each night since. My draxilio knew it immediately. He's told me over and over what you are to me, but I didn't listen. I was stubborn. Foolish."

I suck in a breath, and I'm pretty sure my heart stops.

"Living for the smiles of another never appealed to me until those smiles belonged to you. Now I can't picture my life without them."

He takes a step forward.

"So you can leave," he says. "Run when the pain of life is too heavy for your heart but know this: I'm not letting you go."

Another step as he closes the distance between us.

"If you run, I'll find you. I will be there, ready to carry you when your legs grow tired, because you are *mine*."

It takes a moment for me to realize my whole body is trembling. Every cell in my body urges me forward, but my gaze is stuck on his mouth. That soft, sinful mouth, filled with sharp teeth that bite my skin in all the right places.

A smart girl would return his declaration of love. She would apologize for every fraction of a second she caused him pain, and she'd admit just how long she's felt the same way.

But I'm not a smart girl. So instead, I take a step to the right, toward the sliding door that leads to the patio, a silent challenge in my gaze. "You'll find me, huh?"

He side-eyes me suspiciously. "Yes."

"How long would it take for you to find me?"

His voice lowers to a steady growl. "Not long."

I take another step to the right.

When he sees my gaze dart toward the door, I'm not certain, but it looks like the red part of his eyes starts to blink. Almost like a traffic light. "Don't, Samantha."

"Don't what?" I ask, taking another step.

"Don't run."

I know how easy it is to whip that sliding door open and leap out onto the patio in a full sprint. I've done it dozens of times whenever the familiar jingle of the ice cream truck filled the air.

Rather than waste another second teasing him, I launch myself across the linoleum and throw the sliding door open.

Almost immediately, I'm panting as I charge across the patio, leaping over my mom's potted plants and landing barefoot in the soft grass of the backyard. I don't think it's due to exertion, though. It's because of the primal growl I hear right on my heels, and the heat of his body as he races behind me toward the woods.

"Samantha," he hisses, taunting me.

My pussy clenches at the way he drags out the "ahh" sound at the end. Hot breath fans my neck as I run harder. He's close. He's so close, and I want him to catch me. To slam me against a tree, the rough bark scraping against my back as he tears my clothes into rags and fucks me until I scream.

We make it just inside the tree line at the edge of the cemetery before I'm hurled into the air, my feet leaving the ground as Mylo's strong arms wrap around my middle. He rotates our bodies before we land, and my back slams into his chest as he tightens his grip. As soon as our bodies settle on the ground, we roll away from each other until we're both crouched in the dirt, facing each other with matching feral expressions.

He groans as he takes me in, my nipples hard and aching under my white sports bra. The redness of his eyes sends a chill down my spine. In the woods with him like this, his hair wild and leaves and soil sticking to his clothes, there's nothing human about him. He's all monster. My monster.

In one swift motion, he leaps from a crouched position and lands directly behind me. Before I can react to his impressive agility, he yanks my sweats and booty shorts down my thighs and puts a hand between my shoulder blades, pushing me into the dirt as he lifts my ass in the air.

"Oh, fuck!" I cry out as he parts my cheeks and shoves his tongue between the swollen lips of my pussy.

"Mmm," he groans. "So wet for me."

My hands scramble for purchase as he laps at my core, his tongue relentless in its quest to drink me down. I end up clawing through the dirt until his tongue leaves my pussy and his hands leave my sides. My hips move of their own accord, rolling and bucking as I seek out his touch.

"Mylo," I whimper. But he doesn't leave me for long. I hear the tearing of fabric behind me, then the fat head of his cock pushing through my soaked folds.

He slams into me. It stings, but the pain is quickly buried beneath layers of rippling pleasure, and I can't feel anything but his ridges stretching my insides.

I turn as much as I can to face him, and my pussy flutters at the sight of his curved black horns and the radiant shimmer of his scales. He leans forward and wraps his hand around my neck, lightly squeezing as he holds me in place as he fucks me. My body is no longer mine. It's his to use and fuck and fill with his seed.

"Mylo," I moan, placing my hand over the one that grips my neck. "I don't want kids."

I worry my admission will slow him down, but it doesn't. And if we're really doing this, if we're really solidifying the mate bond and agreeing to spend eternity together, he needs to hear it.

He thrusts harder, faster as he stares deep into my eyes. "Me either," he grunts.

I wipe the dirt from my hand across the front of my bra and reach my other hand between us and play with my clit. "Yesss."

"I...like dogs," he says, timing his words with his thrusts, "and cats."

"Harder," I shout. The slap of his balls against my ass fills the air, and my clit throbs each time I trace a circle around it.

"I...don't like...birds," he adds, growling in approval when he sees the hand between my legs. "No birds."

"No birds," I vow.

His thrusts turn erratic as his speed increases. He's getting close.

My eyes fall closed when my fingers rub my swollen clit side to side. "I-I'm not taking your last name."

He smiles at me, his teeth looking sharper than usual. I want to feel them sinking into my skin. "I'm...not taking...*your* last name."

I almost laugh at his response. He probably doesn't understand what I mean, and the idea of either one of us changing our names to be together must seem ridiculous.

"Samantha," he says, his expression suddenly vulnerable. "Don't... don't run from me."

"Never," I promise, sucking in a breath. My body feels as tight as a bowstring ready to snap. "Not from you." My thighs shake as I press harder into my clit, chasing my release. "Only with you."

A second later, I come. The walls of my pussy clench around him, stroking and milking him, greedy for his seed. "Bite my neck," I whimper, and the moment his teeth break the skin where my neck meets my shoulder, I come again, my vision blurring as his tongue laves the torn flesh.

"I love you, Samantha," he roars as hot come fills my core.

I'm weak, my body sated, and my skin coated in a layer of sweat as I collapse onto the dirt muttering, "I love you too, my dragon mate" as he wraps me in his arms and holds me close. The steady beat of his heart lulls me to sleep.

EPILOGUE

SAM

A MONTH LATER...

"*S*amantha," Mylo calls out, his raspy voice echoing throughout the stone walls of our villa.

"I'm up here," I yell, hoping he can follow the sound of my voice. This place is massive, and every hallway looks the same. I've gotten lost more than once since our arrival last week.

"The car is here to take us into the city center," he hollers. He finds me eventually, wrapping his arms around me from behind and squeezing my stomach. "Mmm, you're so fucking hot," he groans, nibbling the shell of my ear.

"I am, thanks," I reply, cupping his cheek, and showing him the incredible view of the sun bathing the sprawling countryside that I've spent the last hour trying to shoot.

He turns me in his arms, and I gaze up at him, my handsome mate. "You're pretty hot too."

Mylo's brow furrows. "*Pretty* hot?"

I slide his fake glasses off his nose. "Unmask for me," I whisper.

He looks around, and as expected, shakes his head. "I can't. The staff could see. There are too many people here."

"That's on you for renting a lavish Italian villa and hiring an entire household staff to take care of us."

"It's our honeymoon," he reasons. "You want to *cook* and *clean* on our honeymoon?"

I chuckle at his disdain for the two most basic things every human does. "I don't want to cook or clean ever, if we're being honest."

It's not really our honeymoon as we aren't legally married. But we did exchange vows the night we solidified our mate bond. That felt like enough for me. The government doesn't get to decide if my love is valid. I do. So we left it at that and have no plans to do anything else.

The only reason Mylo refers to it as our honeymoon is because this is the first vacation we've taken together. And, of course, since the guy's loaded, he spared no expense when planning our trip to Siena.

He takes my hand and leads me down the stairs to the main floor. Pulling a folded guidebook from his pocket, he flips to a page near the back of the book and points to a section he highlighted. Knowing I don't want to read it, he summarizes for me.

"It says the heart of Siena is divided into seventeen districts, or *contradas*, each with their own flag and mascot. These are used primarily to celebrate the two horse races that take place in the city square each year, but there are themed fountains and museums in each neighborhood and they have community events all year long."

When he flips to the page with the flags, my eyes zero in on one in particular. "Is that a dragon? There's a dragon district?"

He nods, his entire face lighting up with excitement. "There is."

"Okay, well, that's obviously our first stop."

We hop in the back of the car and head through the large, arched gates of the city center, and spend most of the day strolling through the narrow streets of this medieval, gothic paradise. I can't get over how beautiful it is, from the themed lampposts representing the colors and mascots of that particular neighborhood, to the unique black-and-white-striped marble facade of the city's cathedral, to the rich green shutters and flower boxes that seem to adorn every window.

The moment I'm distracted by the stunning details above me, I trip over a cobblestone and remember that Siena is basically a group of small hills and I need to watch where I'm walking. Luckily, the moment my calves and ass get tired from walking uphill, the next street slopes downward, giving my body a break.

By early afternoon, my stomach is growling something fierce, and we stumble into a cute little restaurant in the dragon district since I refuse to eat anywhere else. I'm thoroughly enjoying my red wine and bowl of *cacio e pepe* when Mylo brings up my Mom's condo.

"Do you plan on keeping it?" he asks. "You spend most nights at my house."

I don't know why this has been such a difficult decision for me to make. I never liked that house or the development it's in, and I still can't go up or down the stairs without picturing Mom's fall. On the other hand, my entire childhood took place within those walls. There are bad memories, of course, but also a lot of good ones too.

I picture Mom, long before her diagnosis, cooking dinner in the kitchen while singing along to eighties hairband music. Or the hours she spent tending to the little garden she planted next to the patio. I had a complicated relationship with her, but she loved the hell out of her children. She worked hard and she loved hard.

However, those memories are already with me. I don't need the house to remember how Mom was before the Alzheimer's, and if Mylo and I are going to plant roots in Sudbury and start our lives together, I don't think I want our story to begin in that condo.

"No," I finally say. "I want to sell it."

He reaches for my hand under the table and squeezes. "You are certain? You do not have to decide today."

"I'm certain," I tell him confidently. "Let's get a new place that's just ours, where we can make new memories."

He smiles, and that dimple makes me melt in my seat. "I'd like that."

Suddenly, Mylo drops his fork onto his plate with a clatter and lifts his nose into the air.

"What's wrong?" I ask, noticing how his face has turned two shades paler than it was a second ago.

"I sense...something. A presence."

That sounds ominous. "A presence? What kind of presence?" And because I can't help myself—I blame the wine—I add, "A dragon presence, perhaps?"

He sniffs the air again. "Yes."

At first, I think he's kidding. He has to be kidding. But when his expression remains serious, I shiver. "Wait, what do you mean?"

Pulling out his wallet, he drops a wad of euros on the table and grabs my hand. "We need to leave. Now."

He apologizes profusely to the staff in Italian as he drags me out of the restaurant and sends a text to our driver.

"Is he picking us up?" I ask as we walk-run down the street toward the city gates.

"No," he calls over his shoulder. "I'm getting you outside the walls and we're flying back to the villa."

I want to tug out of his grasp and demand he tells me exactly what's going on because this doesn't make any sense. Does he really sense another dragon here? Is it an alien? Or a dragon shifter that was born on this planet? A dozen more questions float through my mind as we race toward the gates, wine and pasta sloshing around in my tummy and making me regret that second glass of red.

"This doesn't seem like the most efficient way out of here," I shout. My legs are short and my stomach is starting to hurt, but it's not like he can shift in the middle of these crowded, narrow streets either. I don't have a better plan, but I can say with certainty that this one sucks.

"You're right," he says as he stops and hauls me into his arms. Then he starts to run at full speed, and I have to turn my head into his neck to keep the constant jostling from making me sick. It takes several minutes to get outside the gates, but as soon as we do, Mylo finds the nearest copse of trees and heads straight for them.

He takes us to a space in the middle that doesn't seem big enough for him to shift without knocking at least one down, but he seems undeterred as he places me on my feet and shakes out his limbs, readying for the transition. We can't communicate when he's in his dragon form, so the flight back to the villa is quiet. The villa is at the top of a massive hill, so when we reach the bottom, he shifts back, and we climb into one of the parked golf carts that take us to the top.

"Spill it," I say once he gets the cart started. "What happened back there?"

His features are tight as he focuses on the stone path in front of us. "I'm not entirely sure," he says with a sigh. "But we are not alone here."

"What in the galactic fuck does that mean?" I ask. The words come out as a shriek. I take a deep breath to calm down, but it does nothing to soothe my fears. "You sensed another dragon? An alien who is also a dragon or what?"

He rubs a hand down his face. "I don't know. It was the scent, but more than that. I could...feel it. Them."

"I'm sorry, did you say *them*?"

"There is more than one. They felt like me, like me and my brothers but...different. I do not think they are draxilio, but perhaps something like us."

I consider this as he drives us the rest of the way up the hill. More draxilios on Earth, or rather, more alien dragon shifters. It's a scary thought, but only at first. Mylo doesn't know anything about them, so of course, he was going to get me out of there immediately. They could be dangerous. Or they could be exactly like the Monroe brothers— honest, kind, fiercely protective, and just trying to live a quiet life among humans.

If they're anything like Mylo and his brothers, I consider that a win for Earth.

Once we get back to the villa, Mylo seems much calmer. I ask if we need to change our flights and head home early, but he doesn't think it's necessary. "I will sense them before they get close, and I do not sense them now. We are safe here."

"Do you think they could sense you?" I ask.

"Without knowing what they are, there is no way to be sure, but even if they did, we left so quickly, I don't think they could track us."

He pulls out his phone and heads to the bedroom to call Axil to make him aware of the situation, but I hear him reassure Axil that there is no imminent threat, and not to be worried.

Once he's off the phone, I suggest we have a drink on the terrace, and Mylo reluctantly agrees, still a bit shaken by the almost-encounter. It takes three glasses of wine for Mylo's mood to lift, and I'm relieved when the easy smile returns to his face. He cracks open a second bottle of red, and pulls me into his lap as he peppers my face and neck with kisses. I can't tell if it's the romantic vibe of the terrace that's making him cuddly, or the wine, but either way, I don't care.

He can't seem to keep his hands off me. The feeling is mutual. It must be some kind of alien dragon magic because ever since the night we made our mate bond official, I've had this need, this desire, to always be touching or stroking his skin. He feels softer, warmer, I think, and a gnawing hunger fills me whenever we're apart.

"How was your flight this morning?" I ask between sips. "Where'd you go?"

"I hugged the coast then went out over the middle of the sea," he says, his gray eyes filled with wonder. "It's quite beautiful here."

"Mmm," I nod. "Totally agree."

"We should go back tomorrow so you can see it," he suggests.

I love that idea. "Can we find a private beach?" I ask.

"Why a private one?"

"Because I forgot to pack a bathing suit."

His pupils dilate as he drops the bread he's holding onto his plate. "Let's go now."

Such a dude. "You don't have to fly me to a private beach to get me naked, you know."

"Excellent point." He leans back in his chair, the hem of his T-shirt lifting just enough for me to catch a glimpse of the delicious V that points directly to his ridge-covered dick.

My mouth waters at the thought of him taking me right here. Him shoving our wine glasses to the floor in a pile of broken glass as he slams into me over and over.

"Wait, what time is it?" he asks.

"Who cares?" I reply, reaching for his belt.

He chuckles as he pulls his phone out of his pocket. "I want to check on the library. See how Charlie is managing on her own."

"You realize I was about to get naked and fuck you right here on the terrace, right?"

His pupils dilate at my words, and he stares at my mouth for several seconds before leaning down next to my ear and whispering, "The staff is still here. You think I would allow anyone else to gaze upon your magnificent body? You are mine, Samantha." He reaches between my legs, beneath the hem of my dress, and strokes along the seam of my panty-covered pussy. "This is *mine*."

My feminism leaves my body entirely upon hearing the possessive edge in Mylo's voice as he claims ownership over my pussy. He can have it, plant a flag on it, set up an entire society, and even open McDonald's on it if he wants, as long as he keeps talking to me like that.

"Say it," he growls.

His tongue flicks across the pulse point on my neck, sending shivers down my spine. "Yours," I moan. "My pussy is yours."

He reaches for his wine glass and feeds me a sip, his eyes heavy-lidded as they remain locked on me.

We sit like this for a while, me in his lap as we take turns drinking wine from his glass. Eventually, he asks what time it is in New Hampshire.

I quickly do the math in my head. "It's getting late. Think Charlie's still up?"

"Yeah, I think so."

He puts the phone on speaker to make the call. She answers right away. "Hey, boss. How's the honeymoon?"

"Hi, Charlie," I shout.

"Ay, what up, girl?" she replies cheerfully.

"Charlie, how are you?" he asks. "How is the library?"

"Smooth sailing over here," Charlie says. "Uma's free next month, by the way. I spoke with her this morning."

"Wonderful," Mylo says, his smile reaching his eyes at the news. "How are preparations for the *Twilight* trivia night going?"

I say nothing, but inside I'm screaming. *Twilight* was my entire life when the movies came out, and I went on to listen to the audiobooks over and over, never tiring of them. It's somewhat of a secret obsession of mine.

Mylo must be able to tell because he gives me a strange look but continues with his conversation.

"Edward and Bella costumes have been ordered, and I think I've talked the owner of Tasty Tortellini into providing free breadsticks, salad, and pizza for the event."

"I thought they were only willing to give us pizza?" Mylo asks.

"Yeah, well, ya girl sweet-talked them into more freebies."

"Bravo," I say, genuinely clapping. Charlie works so hard. I know it's been nice for Mylo to finally have someone to lean on. "So who are you dressing up as, Charlie?"

"Mmm, I'm not much of a *Twilight* fan," she admits, and I can hear her grimace through the phone. "I'll probably dress up as Alice or something. Then I can hop around and be socially awkward and it won't seem weird."

Aw, now I kinda wish I chose Alice. But being the Bella to Mylo's Edward will also be fun. "Genius."

"Okay, I need to go to bed, and y'all need to get back to your honeymoon."

We say our goodbyes and are about to hang up when Charlie stops us. "I just noticed Zev signed up for my beginner guitar class, by the way."

Mylo and I wear matching furrowed brows. Why would Zev need to take a guitar class when he has the ability to communicate with machines? It took him what? Three days to master the violin?

"I'm looking forward to getting to know him better," Charlie says. "Anyway, have fun!"

She hangs up, and Mylo and I continue to look at each other, puzzled and intrigued.

"What is Zev up to?" I ask with an amused chuckle.

Mylo shakes his head. "I think he may have found his mate."

* * *

Thank you for reading HER ALIEN LIBRARIAN! I hope you loved Mylo and Sam's story. Are you wondering how Zev could pretend to be bad at playing guitar? Or what Charlie's been running from? What about their Happily Ever After?

Good news! You're about to find out!

Zev Monroe abandoned his career as a tattoo artist to pursue his love of music. It might've been a risky decision if he weren't a millionaire alien-dragon shifter whose special power is communicating with machines.

He mastered the violin in four days, so learning the guitar shouldn't take him long, right? The problem is he's developed a major crush on his guitar instructor Charlotte "Charlie" Brooks and pretends to be clueless in order to spend more time in her class.

But Charlie has too much on her plate to even consider pursuing the hot brother of her boss. She's a single mom, she's new in town, and she's constantly looking over her shoulder wondering when her past will catch up to her.

During a night of debauchery, Zev and Charlie end up married, and though neither can remember saying, "I do," they both want to remain in the marriage for different reasons. Charlie wants to maintain sole custody of her daughter, while Zev just wants a chance to prove to Charlie that he's a worthy mate.

Eventually, their worlds collide in dangerous and unexpected ways, and the idyllic small town of Sudbury is forever changed.

Start reading HER ALIEN STUDENT now!

ALSO FROM IVY

ALIENS OF OLUURA

Saving His Mate

Charming His Mate

Stealing His Mate

Keeping His Mate

Healing His Mate

Enchanting Her Mate

(This series isn't finished. There's plenty more to come!)

STRANDED ON EARTH

Her Alien Bodyguard

Her Alien Neighbor

Her Alien Librarian

Her Alien Student

Her Alien Boss (Coming April 2024)

ENJOY THIS BOOK?

Did you enjoy this book? If so, please leave a review! It helps others find my work.

Get all the deets on new releases, bonus chapters, teasers, and giveaways by signing up for my <u>newsletter</u>.

FROM IVY

*H*ow dreamy is Mylo? When I wrote him, I was envisioning a mix of Chidi Anagonye from *The Good Place*, Jessica Day from *New Girl*, Chris Evans (because, duh), and Levar Burton from *Reading Rainbow*. The man loves books, but he also wants to foster a passion for reading in everyone around him because of how much it has impacted his life.

Back on Sufoi, Mylo wasn't a nerd, as none of the draxilios were able to embrace different aspects of their identities. They were assassins who served the king, nothing more. But being able to study the human race from afar—from their history to their art to their mating rituals—provided a path from a life that he hated into a fresh start on a planet where he was allowed to be who he wanted (for the most part).

That's where Sam comes in. She learned that the Monroe brothers were alien dragon shifters in book one, and as you'll recall, she was more concerned they were possible serial killers, so the news that they're just aliens trying to blend in among humans was welcome news to her. When Mylo and Sam hook up throughout the book, Mylo is unmasked, allowing him to be completely himself in his most vulnerable state. It's not just attraction and amazing sex that makes Mylo realize Sam is his mate, it's the friendship they unintentionally build during the course of their fling.

Sam, on the other hand, has built the walls around her heart extremely high, and is much tougher to crack. Her dad left when she was super young, she felt pressured to keep her dyslexia a secret, and has spent the majority of her adult life traveling alone. When she gave marriage a try, it didn't work out, so why would she believe true love exists? Or that having a partner would even make sense with her lifestyle?

It took Sam being forced to come home to a place she hates, to do a job she's terrified of doing, and the death of her mother for her to reevaluate everything. She thought she was running toward success and happiness through her job as a photographer, but she was really running from everything she fears.

Mylo helps her face those fears, and he does so with empathy, kindness, and being a steady presence in her life. He has his possessive alpha moments, but for the most part, he's a gentle hero with an analytical mind, and I love that about him.

Also, you might've noticed the many political threads in this story that are relevant to what's happening in our society. Sorry if it made this book feel heavier than others. I try to provide an escape for my readers into a world that makes you forget what you see on the news. But when the setting is modern-day Earth, it's harder to do that.

Plus, I wrote this during Pride Month, so I let my queer sass take the wheel. *shrug* I'm just tired. Tired of what's happening to the beautiful members of my community, to the ridiculous hate being directed at drag queens, the book bans…all of it. We deserve better.

Speaking of ridiculous hate, I'm sure you're wondering when Officer Burton will get what's coming to him. Don't worry! Karma is on her way. I have big plans for Burton.

Up next is Her Alien Student, aka Zev and Charlie's story! Charlie is also running from her fears (and secrets), and those fears are about to find her in Sudbury. The quiet life she's trying to build is about to crumble, while Zev pretends to be a tone-deaf amateur musician just so he can get closer to Charlie.

Stay tuned!

Love,

Ivy

P.S. - A huge thank-you to my sensitivity reader, Adriana M. Martínez Figueroa. It was an honor to work with you and I'm endlessly grateful for all you taught me about Puerto Rican culture.

The early drafts of my books are truly hideous, and it's only with the help of Tina, Mel, and Jenny, that they turn into beautiful book butterflies. These three angels polish my words and calm my fears, and I'm just an aimless scribbler without them.

P.P.S - Thank you, Peggy Sue Airheart, for fact-checking some of my medical content in a previous draft. I appreciate you!

RESOURCES

The Trevor Project (LGBTQ+ Organization)
1-866-488-7386 (call or chat)
thetrevorproject.org/get-help/

Alzheimer's Association
1-800-272-3900 (call or chat)
https://www.alz.org/help-support/resources/helpline

SAMHSA (Substance Abuse and Mental Health Services
Administration Hotline)
1-800-662-HELP (4357)
TTY: 1-800-487-4889
samhsa.gov

RAINN (Rape, Abuse, & Incest National Network)
1-800-656-4673 (call or chat)
rainn.org

National Suicide Prevention Hotline

1-800-273-8255 (call or chat)
suicideprevention.org

ABOUT IVY

Ivy Knox has always been a voracious reader of romance novels, but quickly found her home in sci-fi romance because life on Earth can be kind of a drag. When she's not lost on faraway worlds created by her favorite authors, she's creating her own.

Ivy lives with her husband and two neurotic (but very cute) dogs in the Midwest. When she's not reading or writing, she's probably watching *Our Flag Means Death*, *Bridgerton*, *Broad City*, or *What We Do in the Shadows* for the millionth time.

Printed in Great Britain
by Amazon

45710877R10109